THANK YOU AND BONUS NOVEL!

I'd like to take a moment to thank you for your ongoing support. You make this all possible! To really show you my appreciation for downloading this book, **I'd love to send you a full-length horror novel in 3 formats (MOBI, EPUB and PDF) absolutely free!**

Download your full-length horror novel, get free short stories, and receive future discounts by visiting www.ScareStreet.com/SaraClancy

See you in the shadows,
Sara Clancy

CHAPTER 1

The cold iron wall of the paddle steamer was an unyielding force at Marigold's back. She pressed against it until her shoulder blades ached and the chill seeped through her sweater. Each breath was a staggered gasp. The blood splattered across her face was cold. It was always cold. But her blood was like fire as it trickled along the shell of her ear. She squeezed her eyes shut and waited for her heartbeat to slow down once more. When she pried her eyelids open, the corpse was still there. Broken and twisted, the mangled body was draped over the round table.

At one time, the room must have been an elegant sight. Far smaller than a normal ballroom. The hall had been used to entertain the guests on the river cruises. The tables were still set into place. Decorations dangled from the high ceiling and they adorned the railing of the second level above. Time had robbed the set-up of all its former beauty. Moss and mold crept over the layers of scum that stained the tablecloths and dripped from the swaying streamers. Blood oozed out from the man, soaking into the greyish tablecloth under him, the stains growing before her eyes. He had just fallen from the balcony above but already the stench of death and rot polluted the room. He always rotted so fast. The man's skin was grey and slick. Half of his face had been destroyed by the impact, reduced to mangled hunks of meat and bone. Yet he was still staring at her. He was always staring at her, every day, no matter where she stood, the whites of his eyes rotting to a sickening brown.

Her fingertips rattled against the rusted wall as she reached above her head, blindly groping for something to hold onto. She found a dent large enough to grab tightly and used it as leverage to pull herself onto her feet. Her knees wanted to buckle and pain pulsed out from the gash over her right temple. Blood trickled over her ear. She brushed the back of her hand over it as she tried to regain her composure.

You should have checked the time, she chastised herself. *This is your own fault.*

For three months it had been the same. A struggle, screaming, and a crash so loud there wasn't a spot on board long or far enough to keep her from hearing it. She knew not to come into the ballroom until after four in the afternoon. She knew. But she had stupidly wandered in nonetheless, eager to get it over with. Louis would be here soon and she didn't want him to see this. Didn't want him to know. She staggered forward, and cautiously approached the corpse. He had never moved before, not after his final death rattle. But it felt like his eyes followed her; watched her. Waiting.

Dust and grime covered the paddle steamer's windows. It turned the afternoon light into a murky brown and even the few broken windows could not salvage a normal shade. Dead leaves and twigs covered the floor. They crunched under her every step. It wasn't exactly what she had envisioned when she had daydreamed of visiting a historic paddle steamer. The others she had seen had looked so beautiful, like a whisper from a time long gone. This one wasn't separated from time. It had been destroyed by it.

Carefully, with her gaze locked on the corpse, Marigold reached down and looped her fingers around the edge of the tablecloth. One quick tug and she was able to cover its face. It was always easier when he wasn't watching her. With practiced efficiency, she pulled up the remaining ends and tied them together as best she could. The result was a sack, with a large knot to hold onto and the corpse nestled inside. Blood still seeped out. It dripped on the floor with rhythmic thuds, like the ticking of a clock. She was taking too long. *Louis will be here soon. He'll see.* She couldn't let him know.

Crouching down, she placed her hands over the rim of the table and pushed up. Her slender arms struggled to lift the weight of the corpse. They trembled with the strain as the table inched up. It toppled over with a sudden swish and a deafening crash. The sound echoed off the walls and rebounded within her chest. The bundled corpse skidded across the floor, trapping the foliage debris against the slick material while blood smeared across the floor. Leaving the table on its side, she scurried around to grab the knot. It was heavy. It was always so heavy. Her shoulders strained and the soles of her shoes squeaked as she pulled it across the floor. No matter how many times she did this, she never got used to the weight.

There was a door on the far side of the room, wide enough to keep up with the aesthetics of the ballroom, that opened out onto a balcony. Each of the four levels of the paddle boat had matching balconies, with the lower two levels hanging out significantly further than the top two. The ballroom was on the fourth floor, with only the captain's cabin and steering house above. Each day the man fell through the sunroof. She always heard the glass break, but there was never any glass when she came in.

She was out of breath by the time she managed to tug the bundle out through the door. Life would have been much easier if she could toss it over the railing from here, but she was never strong enough to lift it. She had to get it down the spiral staircase to the second floor. Taking a moment, she rested against the railing of the balcony. It consisted of three lower poles with large gaps between them, and a strip of wood at hip height. Red paint chipped off the splintering surface, but it was still sturdy enough to carry her weight. She took a deep breath, the air tainted with the dusky but sweet scent of Spanish moss and rolled her shoulders. Not able to wait any longer, she went back to work.

Sweat glistened on her skin by the time she got the corpse to the top of the spiral staircase. Her mind shifted rapidly between focused and reeling. She was able to stop her thoughts from wandering. *Why couldn't they have kept to the concepts of a straight staircase? Were spirals really that more appealing?* It wasn't easy to maneuver her bulky package through it, so she had taken to tossing it down in short bursts. She squirmed with each resounding contact against the railing. Some were accompanied with a wet squish, others with a crack of bone, but each time her stomach churned. There was no dignity in the process. She hadn't known him in life yet didn't doubt that he deserved more reverence to be taken with his body. But it wasn't really his body, not anymore. In all of the campfire stories she had heard growing up, she had never known that ghosts could do this. That they could come back physically. Or could have their remains become a physical presence. She clung to that thought as she was forced to kick him again to get him down further. It wasn't really him.

The steps groaned under their combined weight, the metal they were connected to releasing rusted shrieks. By the time they reached the next floor, her legs were screaming and sweat drizzled along her spine. The blood was still seeping from her forehead. The neckline of her sweater was stained and slick, and stuck against her shoulder. She grabbed onto the railing and sunk down onto the balcony floor next to the sack. An empty hollow feeling had swallowed up her insides.

Resting her unmarred temple against a pole, Marigold looked out over the thick layer of emerald green moss that blanketed the swamp. Spindly trees reached out with branches like skeletal fingers, clawing out of the ever-present fog which clung to the bayou floor. On bright days like these, it was possible to see the far bank, sometimes even a bit further. On other days, it was impossible to see past the balcony. The bayou was never really quiet. Frogs and bugs joined together to create a constant symphony. Every so often, something would thrash under the water, heard but unseen. A fish or a snake, maybe an alligator or two.

She never knew what happened to the bodies once she had surrendered them to the murky water of the bayou. But each day the body was back, reappearing on the same table in the ballroom. *Was it the same body, over and over?* she thought. *Or did they just pile up under the water?* Since she had never been brave enough to enter the water, she never had any answers. Just questions in her head and a sick feeling in her stomach.

The soft rumble of a car engine snapped her back into the moment.

Louis. It couldn't be. She still had hours. *Why was he so early?* she thought wildly. It couldn't be anyone else. No one ventured this far into the bayou unless they were very lost. She ran to the side of the boat that was nestled alongside the muddy bank. It overlooked the only place possible to park a car, even though half of it would be swallowed by the incoming tide. Her fingers twisted around the top rail, the wood splintering in her grip.

The boat was beached in a wide clearing that was almost impassable, and dangerous if you didn't know where to step. There were wide patches of soft mud that could easily bog a car. In other places, the floating grass was thick enough that it looked like solid land. Louis had told her stories of people who had stepped onto it and been swallowed whole; the grass would instantly close up, trapping the person underneath. Unless there was someone there who knew exactly where you had gone in, there wasn't much of a chance you were getting out again.

With these conditions, there was only one possible route the car could be coming from. Unfortunately, it was closely bracketed by a cluster of trees that tapped the fog, making it thicker. She peered into the grey blanket, frantically searching for a hint of a vehicle. But there was no way she was going to see him, not until he was a few yards away.

He can't see this. Marigold ran back to the corpse and hurled it towards the next flight of stairs. The noise grew louder as she finally reached it. She kicked at it with all her strength, forcing it down the staircase, but it kept getting trapped in the curves and bannister posts. Blow after blow, she fought for each inch with sweat and panic. The soft purr of the engine rose into a roar. With one last kick, the body toppled out onto the deck. On this floor, down at the other end of the ship, there was a hole in the railing. She knew from experience that it was large enough to fit the bundle through, but if Louis made it up to the deck, she wouldn't have any cover. If she wasn't fast enough, Louis would see. *He can't see. He can't know.*

Her fingers ached to the point of breaking as she fisted them into the tablecloth. The weight pulled her down, made each step tiny and hurried. All the muscles in her back clenched, her arms trembled, and she couldn't pull in a full breath. She made it to the front of the boat in time to see twin lights begin to emerge from the fog. Marigold almost fell as she threw herself back, using her body weight to move the bundle. The car engine blared. Reaching back with one hand she grabbed the twisted railing and used it as leverage to pull herself closer. The mud sloshed and squished under rolling tires.

Her heart hammered against her ribs, she shoved the body into the gap. It clung to the edges, the blood-soaked material damp against her hands. She threw her shoulder against it, her legs skidding over the deck. With a sudden jolt and a rip of fabric, the bundle slipped through. She almost fell with it. The air rushed from her lungs as she slammed against the deck, half of her torso dangling through the gap. It fell into the water with a loud splash and quickly disappeared. The floating moss rippled and swayed on the waves. Then the vibrating green moss drew together once more, concealing the water and the corpse it now held. Relief settled into her stomach as she slid herself back onto the boat. Then she noticed the blood.

CHAPTER 2

Long thick strips of blood streaked over the deck, a visible track of every inch the body had travelled. Her ribs throbbed as she stripped off her sweater and hurriedly began to mop up the blood stains. All the thin nylon did was push the crimson liquid around. A car door slammed shut and she flipped her head up. Without a thought, she pushed her hand through her hair, only noticing the blood on her hands afterwards. She told herself that it was okay. Her natural hair color would hide most of it.

She threw her sweater to the side, as far along the back of the boat as she could. There was some outdoor furniture on the front deck, a little sitting area Louis had arranged in an attempt to make the place seem a bit more welcoming. She made it across the place just as Louis jogged up the makeshift gangplank. He met her eyes and a soft, easy smile spread across his face.

"Well, hey there, Cher!" His southern drawl was sweet and husky and soothed the panicked core of her being.

But Louis Dupont was an observant man, and it didn't take more than a second for him to notice something was off. He didn't hesitate to rush towards her.

"I'm okay," she said hurriedly. "I just fell over and cracked my head. It's not bad."

He didn't believe her for a second, she could see it in his eyes, but he nodded and forced a smile again. With gentle fingers, he nudged at her chin to get a better look at her temple.

"Did you hit your head on anything metal? We might have to give you a tetanus shot."

"No, it was a tabletop."

Again, he watched her carefully but didn't comment.

"Well, let's get you patched up."

She grabbed his wrist and started to pull him towards the back door, careful to take him through a route that would keep him away from the trail of blood. He quirked an eyebrow at the contact. They hadn't touched for a long time.

For a while, it seemed that the only time people reached out for her was to hurt her. It made her weary. She was never sure if Louis had put a conscious effort into it, but he naturally kept the perfect distance away, nicely on the edge of her comfort zone.

"I've got the first aid kit in the kitchen," she said by way of explanation.

"Okay." Suspicion hung heavily in his voice. "Lead the way."

Marigold released his wrist but kept her eyes on him, worried that he might dash off to the side any second to investigate. But she needn't have worried. Louis fell into step behind her and patiently followed her to the lower deck. The kitchen was towards the back of the boat. Even with all the dumbbell waiters that had once lifted the food to the dining hall and further on to the ballroom, it still must have been a pain for anyone who had worked on the ship in its prime. Before a hurricane had promptly relocated it into the inland swamps.

It must have been beautiful when it was first built. A classic paddle streamer designed to let people travel the Mississippi River in style. When the fog thickened and the tide rolled in, it almost looked like it once had. At that time, it looked like it was floating. But eventually the tide receded and the boat was once again left abandoned in the reeds.

Only a few stubborn guests and staff had refused to leave as the storm had brewed. She didn't know the exact number, but she knew that four of them remained here. They couldn't leave, not until they were willing to cross over to whatever existed beyond this world. All things considered, Marigold supposed that they had taken well to her becoming their new shipmate. But that didn't mean that they didn't keep the bowels of the ship as cold as a meat locker. She hunched her shoulders against the chill as Louis followed her to the kitchen.

"So, how are things going?" Louis asked.

Marigold was careful in her answer. Louis had taken her under his wing, partly because of their shared history, and partly because she so desperately needed someone to care for her. Louis had a strong protective instinct and didn't shy away from doing all he could to help her. He was the kind of man who would throw himself towards danger if it would spare someone else from pain.

The paddle steamer had been his idea. The demon that had attached itself to her had been gathering strength and she had needed some place safe. Somewhere the demon couldn't follow. With a few territorial ghosts in residence and the addition of the voodoo charms Louis's mother had placed around the boat, this place was like a walled castle. Not completely impenetrable, but considerably safer. Louis wasn't naive by any measure, so she never could decide if he truly believed that the demon would give up if its access was cut off. She didn't believe it, but she never told him that.

"As good as can be expected," she eventually answered.

"And what did you trip over again?"

Marigold smiled over her shoulder. "Okay, okay. One startled me and I tripped. But it was my fault."

Louis grabbed her wrist to make her stop walking. The afternoon light caught his glasses and gave extra light to his hazel eyes.

"None of this is your fault. You don't deserve any of what's happening to you."

She blushed and tried to shrug in his grip. "Well, when you consider my family, this might be karma."

"No, it's not. That's not even how karma works. Unless you're saying that you're a reincarnation of one of your own ancestors."

Sighing dramatically, Marigold rolled her eyes. She should have known better by now. There were a few subjects that you just couldn't take lightly around Louis. Having grown up in a family of voodoo practitioners and paranormal investigators, Louis took certain subjects way too seriously. It was a lesson she had learned after using the terms 'ghost orb' and 'ghost vortex' interchangeably. Louis had enthusiastically explained the vast differences for almost two hours.

She cut him off before he could get started on the finer details of reincarnation. "It's a figure of speech. I just meant that I knew better. Mr. Smash Mouth causes a fuss in the same room, at the same time, every day. I should have just let him do his thing."

"Mr. Smash Mouth?"

Marigold froze for a moment before she entered the kitchen. "After the singer."

She didn't look back to see if he believed the lie. An image of the broken body flashed again in her mind. Blood. Pearly bones cracked through tender flesh. Broken teeth and hanging eyeballs. Each day the ghost's face was pulverized anew, but it was his destroyed mouth that she remembered the most. So, Mr. Smash Mouth it was. It made it easier to deal with the situation. A lot easier than knowing the man's real name. The kitchen had once been a marvel of industrial steel, but now only patches of that grandeur remained. She reached into one of the cabinets and groped around for the first aid kit. Its bright red case was probably the only pristine thing in the room, including herself.

Louis looked over the room as he moved to the counter. "What happened to the cabinet doors?"

"Oh," she fixed a smile into place before she turned back again. "One of them really likes banging doors. After the eighth consecutive hour, I decided that it was enough."

He gestured to the pots and pans that littered the floor and threw her a quizzical look. When he knelt down to pick them up, she spoke.

"Don't bother," she said.

Curiosity sparked in his eyes, something mischievous and childlike, and it made her smile turn real. "Okay, fine. Pick up a few and put them here." She tapped her fingers against a spot on the counter and retreated to the door. "Then duck."

He placed the pots in his hands where she had indicated. The pots had already begun to rattle before he had a chance to pack up. The sound of clattering metal ricocheted around the room as the pots trembled violently. They flung off of the counter, straight at his head. Louis ducked and they collided with the wall an inch above his head, hard enough to dent both the wall and the pans. The room echoed with the noise. Then, with a grinding slide, the pans slid back where Louis had picked them up from. Louis remained hunched, surprise evident on his face. Slowly, with mounting composure, he pushed his dark-framed glasses higher onto his nose and straightened up.

"Okay." A smile quirked his lips. "Why have you not told me about that?"

Marigold unzipped the first aid kit and retrieved a bottle of iodine and a bunch of cotton wool balls. "I thought I had."

"I would have remembered this level of poltergeist activity."

She shrugged and handed him the small bottle. "It's not like it's an issue. They like their mess and I don't want to clean up after them. It's a special kind of harmony."

He reached out to take the items from her hands, his larger fingers dwarfing her own, and she was caught up once again by the vast difference in their skin tones. She hadn't really noticed it until her Aunt had attempted to kill them. The devastation of that night had left her hovering between life and death and heavily drugged. She remembered how, with morphine in her system, his dark skin had shone with the strength of the moon. Like dark, rich, polished tiger's eye gemstones. She always looked sickly pale in comparison and almost fevered with her clusters of red freckles. Once more with a feather light touch, he twisted her head to the side to study her wound. The bleeding had stopped.

"It doesn't look that bad," he mused.

"That's what I said."

He pulled back and caught her gaze. "So where did all the blood on your hands come from?"

No matter how hard she tried, she couldn't keep from squirming.

"Nothing bleeds like a head wound."

The strong scent of antiseptic burned her nose as he doused the cotton wool with iodine. Despite his warning, the first touch was a surprise. Each dab was a sharp sting into her skull and she felt stupid for wincing. This was hardly the worst pain that she had ever endured. The scar that sliced across the middle of her neck was a testament to that. Each time she thought about it, of her father opening her skin with a kitchen knife, she could almost feel the blade again. Her parents had both been nurses. They had told her about phantom pains, about how amputees could sometimes feel an ache in a limb they didn't have anymore. Sometimes the scar felt like that, like an ache that would never really go away, no matter how well it healed.

"Maggie?"

She blinked rapidly and looked up to meet Louis's eyes. His Clark Kent-like glasses framed his face rather well and made his hazel eyes brighter.

"Sorry, I must have tuned out."

He frowned. "Maybe we should take you to a hospital."

"I'm okay," she replied, but her protests didn't clear the concern from his expression. "I don't have a concussion."

He began to pack the items away. "I'll believe half of that. Which half do you want to pick?"

Marigold snatched the first aid kit out of his hand and put it back on the shelf. "I'm adjusting."

From his position by the door, Louis watched her every move. She could feel his eyes drifting over her exposed skin, assessing each new cut and bruise. In some places, her skin had become so discolored that it hid her freckles. She washed her hands in the pump action sink, watching the bloodstained water swirl down the drain.

"I brought food," he said abruptly. "But how about we go out tonight? Hit the town?" She cocked an eyebrow and he smiled. "Okay, okay. Hit the few buildings that have been strategically placed around a road. Come on, Cher. I hear the food ain't that bad."

The whole boat heaved and rattled as a ghastly wail echoed through the corridors. Out of the small window, she watched the last rays of sunlight paint the sky a sickly pink.

"They're waking up."

"Ghosts are naturally more active at night," Louis said, as if there was any comfort to it.

She dried her hands on her jeans and realized that blood still covered her shoulder, her hair, and half of her face.

"Okay," she mumbled. "Just let me get changed."

***

The issue hadn't just been to find a haunted place for Marigold to stay in. That would have been far easier. New Orleans has a way of holding onto things that other places released like a whispered sigh. The issue had been finding the right kind of ghosts. In his experience, people had heard enough about the 'barrier between life and death' that they could accept the concept even when they didn't believe in an afterlife. It was a lot harder to explain how life and death were more like different ends of a spectrum, rather than dueling forces. 'Ghost' was a general term that covered a lot more than an outsider would consider. And for their purposes, they needed some very specific ghosts.

The demon that had latched itself onto Marigold's family had been allowed to nourish itself with time and blood. It was strong. Strong enough to break through the boundaries that Louis's mother had set into place. But ghosts could be strong, too. And just as territorial. The ghosts that lingered here served as an extra protection for Marigold. His mother liked to refer to them as 'spiritual guard dogs,' but it wasn't entirely accurate. Guard dogs weren't supposed to attack the people they were protecting.

Louis wandered out onto the back deck, torch in hand. It was problematic to have generators out here, and costly. Since they would be leaving shortly, he wasn't inclined to go to the trouble of starting it up. He washed the beam over the large blades at the back of the boat. They had once powered the boat through the water. Now they were chipped and weathered. Broken remains of something that had once been beautiful.

A shrill cackle made him turn. He aimed the beam of his flashlight over the shadows beyond the boat. The mist glowed in his torchlight, as opaque as falling ash. Spanish moss hung in thick tendrils from the trees, swinging like serpents, but Louis couldn't feel a breeze. The laughter came again; a painful shriek that carried on with a child's abandonment. He knew the sound and backed up a little closer to the entrance. *Dubbies* might have a more comical sounding name, but history proved time and again that they weren't ghosts to be dismissed. Not if you wanted to remain as alive as when you started.

He searched the shadows again, his torchlight barely able to penetrate the darkness. Something sloshed through the water. Louis spun to the sound and the small circle of light fell upon a shifting shadow. The dubby stood on the far bank, shadowed under the branches of a willow tree. Grotesquely rotted, but still with all of its limbs, the dubby grinned at him. A feral flash of fangs that twisted up its whole face. Louis felt a deep chill roll over his skin and instinctively patted his pocket. He had always carried a gris-gris for protection while leading paranormal tours around the heart of New Orleans. But since he had met Marigold, he kept the little spell pouch close at all times.

The familiar shape against his palm helped steady his heartbeat. He waited to see what the dubby would decide. Were they just to have a passing encounter or was this destined to be something more violent? Slowly, the dubby rose its hand, its fingers as spindly as a spider's legs. It swayed its forearm in a broken wave. Louis let his hand drift up to mirror the movement. Its smile remained firmly in place as it drifted back into the shadows, its feet never touching the ground.

"Was that the dummy?"

Louis jerked and whipped around. Marigold squinted and held up a hand to protect her eyes from the glare or his torchlight.

"Dubby," he replied after a thick swallow. "Has he been coming by often?"

"He likes standing under that tree."

The spot she indicated was in the distance, but still far too close for his comfort.

"Does it ever come closer?"

"Not really. It just smiles and waves."

"Tell me if it ever gets closer," he said. "Dubbies have the temperament of a two-year-old. They're happy until they're not."

She nodded. "At this point, the other ones worry me more."

He forced a smile and gently curled an arm around her shoulder. She leaned into him just a little, just enough for him to know that she really needed the reassurance. She had lost weight again.

"Remember the plan. The dubby is more concerned with the ghosts on the boat. The ghosts on the boat are more concerned with the dubby."

"And the tension keeps the demon from wanting to step into the middle of it," she finished for him.

Each time he had to remind her, the words lost a little more of their strength, and he was worried that one day they would be rendered useless. She needed something to cling to. Something to keep her strong. The demon had made their battleground about perseverance, defiance, and strength of will. If she faltered, there might not be anything he could do to save her.

CHAPTER 3

The Ragin' Cajun was the only restaurant in town, and the small but sturdy wooden building was always crowded. The deck was on stilts over the water of the bayou, with a stomach-high railing and long thin tables. Weeping willows, dripping with Spanish moss, surrounded the area, while strings of colorful paper lanterns draped from the bare beams. Newspapers were used instead of tablecloths, and each table was lined with bench seats.

Kids ran around like screaming typhoons while a live bluegrass band played in the corner. All the songs were traditionally Cajun, with energetic beats and a strong bass. All the songs were in French, so Marigold didn't understand a word of it, but they sounded nice. It was late October, yet the winter chill didn't stop many from heading out onto the deck. Marigold was grateful for the shift in temperature. She hadn't done well with the stifling heat when she had first arrived in Louisiana. At least now she could tolerate wearing jeans and light jackets again. And the more wounds she covered, the less odd looks she got. In her only act of defiance on this account, Marigold had stopped wearing scarves. After the night with Delilah, after everything really, she didn't care if anyone saw the prominent scar across her neck. It was a reminder that she had survived, and sometimes that was all anyone could do.

There were few things in life that Louis loved as much as food. His eyes would light up at the very mention of it. He led her through the crowd with a smile on his face and a happy bounce in his step. Picking a table near the water's edge, he was practically jumping with excitement and snatched up the menu. It had been a while since she had seen him this happy, and she took a second to appreciate it.

"Do you want crabs, bugs, or crawfish?" He turned over the menu and his jaw dropped. Sheer joy flooded his eyes. "They have a sample platter. We can get all three."

Marigold laughed and shook her head. "Whatever you want. My treat."

Aunt Delilah might have been a sadistic psychopath, but she had possessed the foresight to keep the ancestral home insured. As the last La Roux, Marigold had been the sole beneficiary. There had been a lot of complications. When Delilah had been exposed as a serial killer—a trait that ran thick through the La Roux line—there were a lot of angry people. The person handling the insurance policy had tried to use the horrible public opinion as leverage not to pay out. They had said that since it was arson, which, technically, it was, they didn't owe her a dime. Marigold argued that when the options were starting a fire or getting stabbed to death, the decision was legitimate. But then Joe, Louis's cousin, who also happened to be a police officer, had stepped in. She didn't know what he had said, but things had wrapped up relatively quickly after that. She had her inheritance, and since she was living on a haunted shipwreck in the middle of the bayou, she hadn't made much of a dent in the relatively meagre sum.

Louis's attention flicked over her wrists and his humor faded. The shackles Delilah had used on her had damaged them considerably. Time had soothed the color back to her natural pale shade, but the scars were never going to fade away. She pulled her sleeves down to spare him the sight.

"They don't hurt anymore," she assured.

"That's good."

"How is your arm?"

He had been injured that night as well. But he was a good healer and recovered quickly. From time to time his shoulder joint still ached. Delilah had sliced him along his upper arm. Luckily it hadn't caused any lasting damage, but he now had a long, thin scar that would never go away. Absently, he rubbed it through his long-sleeved shirt.

"I think it adds a little bit of danger to my appearance," he said with a smile.

"Very macho," she agreed.

Laughter and music hung in the air as readily as the scents of spice and melted butter. Marigold could feel the vibrant energy curling around her, comforting and smothering at the same time. It had been days since her last contact with a living person. And at least a month since she had seen anyone but Louis. She wasn't comfortable around anyone else anymore. She didn't trust herself with anyone other than him. One of the demon's favorite pastimes was tormenting her family members until she agreed to kill just to make it stop, if only for a little while. Her genetic history proved that anyone could be dangerous when they were desperate enough.

"We should do this more," Louis said.

Marigold met his eyes. "We haven't even tried the food yet."

"I mean we should get out more. Maybe even go bowling. We spend way too much time in that place."

"That place is my lovely home," she smirked. "Besides, it's dangerous for me to be out here."

He held onto his smile, although it did change into something softer. "I know you're scared, and I'd be lying if I told you there was no reason for you to be. But you need to have social contact. Isolation isn't your friend."

She didn't say anything.

"Maggie, it's important you keep fighting."

"It doesn't seem much like fighting," she admitted.

"Just because it's not physical doesn't mean it's not a fight. Remember the stages of possession. We want to keep it in the infestation stage, not let it get bad enough to be oppression."

It seemed odd that only a year ago she would have had no idea what he was talking about. Only a few months separated her from a normal, happy, oblivious life. Now, she knew how to make protection gris-gris and which prayers to say before she went to bed. She drank holy water and had a blessed rosary around her neck. Now she knew the stages of demonic possession intimately.

Manifestation, infestation, oppression, and possession. Manifestation, the point when someone invites a demon into their lives, had passed before she had been born. When she had met Louis, the demon had almost reached the oppression stage. She had felt the strain of her mind breaking in two, leaving her vulnerable and beaten, and ready to just give up.

It was like having a stalker. One that could be anywhere, saw everything, and could rip apart her mind to find her deepest fears. At first, the goal had been to get rid of the demon completely. Now they just wanted to keep it out of her body. Loud bumps in the night, twisted nightmares, hallucinations, and constant fear of what it would do next had somehow become a 'win' in this scenario. She couldn't remember when the focus had shifted.

"It's going to be angry," she muttered.

Before he could respond, their server came to the table. The middle-aged woman kept casting sidelong looks at Marigold, her attention drifting over the bruises that couldn't be hidden. One of her 'roommates' had gotten out of hand yesterday, and she still had a black eye to show for it. It looked far worse as the bruise blended with dark bags under her eyes.

The waitress spoke French, so Marigold couldn't tell exactly what she was saying, but fear was pretty distinctive in any language. The words flowed from the woman's mouth, no matter how much Louis tried to reassure her. He gave their order and the woman practically ran away the first chance she got.

"Am I still on the news?" Marigold asked as she watched the retreating woman.

"No, the press has died down. Although the ruins of the La Roux home is now a major draw for paranormal tours. It gets pretty crowded."

"Good to know."

"Oh, and a reporter has been trying to get in contact with you. They want to interview you about Delilah. And your parents probably."

"Probably?"

"Well, the segment is going to be called '*My Life Among Killers*', so I can only assume it will cover them, too."

Marigold rolled her eyes. She guessed it was an improvement from the news anchor that had invited her onto their show. He had obviously wanted to blindside her on national television. She couldn't blame them. Not knowing you were living with prolific murderers once is suspicious. People don't want to believe it could happen twice.

"What did you tell them?"

He shrugged one shoulder. "That you're not available for comment."

"You know, it's almost enough to make me feel fascinating." She frowned as a thought hit her. "Did you just purposefully distract me from the waitress?"

A hint of guilt flashed across his face. "Maybe."

"What's going on?" She looked around and noticed that they had garnished the attention of a few guests. They all looked away when she met their gaze.

"It's nothing, really," he said. "It's just, well, there are a lot of ghosts in the bayous, Cher. People here have seen a lot more. They're willing to believe a lot more."

"They know about the demon?"

He cleared his throat and made the face he always did when trying to figure out how best to sugar coat the facts. "Some here see demons as being contagious. You hang out with a marked person long enough and the demon will come after you, too."

Her spine instantly straightened. "Is that possible?"

"It's an old legend." That sentiment was long past having any measure of comfort.

They sat in silence until the woman brought them their drinks. Marigold had quickly grown a taste for sweet tea. It was practically liquid sugar, and she drank way more of it than she should have. It was probably a sign that her growing addiction was showing when Louis had ordered it for her without discussion. The night air was chilled, but still, droplets of condensation covered the glass. She played with them as she thought.

"Maybe you shouldn't hang around me anymore."

"I was actually going to suggest the opposite," Louis said, calmly sipping his soda. "It probably wasn't the best idea to leave you alone for so long."

"Cordelia would have killed you if you had ducked out on her wedding," Marigold pointed out. Her stomach clenched as she cupped the glass with both hands. "I haven't even asked how it was."

"Good. The young bride was blushing, the slightly less young groom was smiling, and we all ended up barefoot on the dance floor."

"Sounds fun."

"Is this when I remind you that you could have gone?"

Most of the Dupont family had an, albeit legitimate, dislike for Marigold. Because of her, Louis had been beaten, stabbed, and had almost been burned alive. Southern hospitality and pity could only go so far. Cordelia was one of the few that actually seemed to like her. The offer to come along to the wedding was a nice gesture, but Marigold was pretty sure the woman knew that she would decline.

"No bride actually wants last minute additions to the wedding they've been planning for months."

"I can't argue with that," Louis said. "I made your apologies. Told her you were far too busy being dark and brooding and deeply mysterious."

He leaned back to give the waitress enough room to place the large bowls of food on the table. In each one, bright shelled crustaceans sat in steaming broths, each rich with scents and spice. Once it was done, there was barely any room left on the table, and in addition to the standard cutlery, they were given mallets and what looked like oversized nutcrackers. Louis instantly pulled one of the bugs out, laid it out on the newspaper, and began to smash it open with a vengeance. Marigold gingerly pulled one of the bugs out of the soup. She wasn't as skilled as him at it and ended up squishing shards of the shell into the meat.

"You know what occurred to me on the drive up?" Louis dunked a strip of the meat into the sauce before swallowing it down. "You have yet to go on a bayou tour. That just seems wrong."

"I've learned as I've gone."

Louis shrugged as he used his hands to crack and rip his way through the shell. "It's not the same unless you've been on an airboat. We should go."

"And this wouldn't be an attempt to make me socialize more?"

"I neither confirm nor deny." With three smooth whacks, he opened up a crayfish and passed it to her. "There's also a plantation around here that does tours. They advertise that you can step back into the good old days. So you just know they're going to ignore the generations of horror and abuse. Keep it family friendly."

Marigold mirrored his early use of the sauce and instantly grabbed her drink as hot peppers exploded across her tongue. Her eyes watered as she struggled to breathe past the burn. Eventually, it subsided enough for her to glare at him.

"That's the only hot one, I swear."

She coughed and wiped her eyes with a napkin, wincing as she pushed too solidly on a bruise.

"So," she croaked. "Why tours?"

"I like nature and have a healthy respect for history."

"You give tours for a living," she said. "Why would you want to take them on your days off?"

"Because I don't have to lead them. I get to be the one to ask stupid questions, touch things I shouldn't, and continuously wander off."

She smiled. "I didn't know you had such a bitter streak."

"I hide it well under passive-aggressive charm."

Marigold smiled, picked a fat looking crayfish, and brought the hammer down into its crimson shell with a sharp crack. The table shook with the blow and rattled against the floorboards. That's when she felt it. A tiny little hand wrapping around her ankle. Brow furrowed, she ducked down to look under the table. Each muscle in her body locked into place before her mind caught up with what she was seeing.

"Louis." Her voice was barely a whisper, but it was enough to entice a threatening hiss from the thing that was under the table.

It wrapped an arm around her ankle, her tiny clawed hand digging into her skin. It looked like a child, an infant, but warped and twisted. Its eyes were too large, the irises like curdled milk. Its skin cracked as it moved. With pointed teeth and a mangled jaw, it looked like something both dead and demonic. And it was inches from her face. Across the underside of the table, she caught sight of Louis as he ducked down to see what had captured her attention. His jaw hung slack, and that was more disturbing than the thing clinging to her leg. He saw it too. How could he see it too?

"Just stay very still, Cher."

"Okay." The word was barely a choked gasp, but the baby's hand tightened like a vice. It drew itself closer until she could smell the reek of Sulphur on its breath.

"And maybe not speak."

The muscles of her sides began to ache, straining against the odd angle, as Louis stood up. It didn't pay him any attention. It only stared at Marigold, so close now that she could barely see its hand. It took all her strength to not move as it reached for her and tangled its talons in her hair. Louis crouched down at the end of the table, trying to keep the curious waitress from edging closer.

She could hear a flurry of French, the same words repeated with increasing volume. The disgusting humanoid smiled at her. Saliva and rot dripped from its fangs. Out of the corner of her eyes, she saw more people duck down to look under the table. Then the screaming began. The creature lunged at her, hitting her with more weight than it should have possessed. She rocked back with the force and toppled from the seat. The air rushed from her lungs as her back collided with the deck. The creature clawed at her face and neck, each blow like fire.

The music halted. Her own screams were lost in the panic of the crowd. She clawed at the tiny frame, struggling to get it off of her. Then the pain vanished, the pressure lifted, and she was left staring up at Louis and the gathered crowd. She thrashed around to check every possible lurking space, but the child was gone. A steady murmur ran through the crowd. It took her a moment to recognize it as whispered prayer. Louis crouched down next to Marigold and gently placed a hand on her shoulder. Normally, the touch would anchor her; help her sort out reality from the hallucinations. This time, it wasn't enough.

"You saw it too," she gasped. "It wasn't just me."

"I saw it," he glanced up at the gathered crowd. She could feel their fear as they carefully kept a wide berth. "And we weren't the only ones."

It wasn't possible. The demon had never been able to pollute other people's minds with its lies. Only hers. Only ever hers. Louis shifted his hand to try and coax her to sit up. They both knew what this meant, but she felt like she needed to hear it admitted out loud.

"It's getting stronger."

CHAPTER 4

Streetlights didn't exist this far into the wastelands. The night closed in on all sides, broken only by the slither of the moon and the high beams of Louis's car. They had left as soon as they could. The server had piled their food into to-go bags and had practically thrown it at them, too scared to get closer. Marigold had left a generous tip, but she still doubted they would ever seat her again. The radio struggled to keep hold of a station. It was impossible to tell what song was playing through the layers of static. Louis had insisted that she drive. Marigold knew there had to be an ulterior motive behind the decision, but she couldn't quite decide which one it was. Either he was trying to give her some sense of control, or he wanted his hands free so he could continue to stuff his face.

He seemed to take it as a personal challenge to open the crustaceans by hand. It was a messy struggle and she was sure Louis was exaggerating the situation to make her laugh. On the few occasions that he was actually successful, he would split the food with her, always dunking it in the sauce first, which just spread the mess.

"Pull over," he said suddenly.

"Why?"

"I want a rock." His eyes narrowed on the crayfish. "I'm gonna smash this sucker open."

"Against what?" she laughed.

"I have a perfectly good dashboard."

"Your car is going to smell horrible tomorrow." She still pulled the car onto the shoulder of the road, just to call his bluff.

"I can wash the car."

"And you can wait to eat until we get back to the boat."

He scrunched up his face. "Cher, where do you pick up that kind of nonsense?"

She cut off the engine but kept the headlights on. The small overhead light clicked on as Louis opened his door, but he couldn't get out of the car until he had passed the mountain of containers, all of which he had opened, over to her. When he was finally free, he leaned through the open passenger door to throw her a triumphant smile.

"You look way too proud of yourself," she noted.

He dramatically rolled his eyes and ducked away. Beyond the impenetrable shadows that clung to the sides of the car, she could hear the soft lapping of water and frogs croaking. She had grown to find the sound peaceful and relaxed into the quiet. Despite whatever carefree facade Louis showed her, she knew that he was already mulling over the new event, cataloguing and scrutinizing. He would find the key points, discuss it with his voodoo queen mother, decide the next step, and only then tell her what they should do. She wasn't practically happy with the practice, but she understood why he did it. The demon was connected to her. Her fear, her anxiety, her anger, it fed off of it all. If she fell apart, she was just feeding it, giving it strength, so he tried to shield her from any anxiety that he could.

Framed by the headlights, Louis kicked at the road in search of an appropriate stone. Tension had just seeped from her shoulders when the silence was shattered by a haunting wail. Marigold jumped as Louis spun around, looking past the car with a spark of fear. She twisted in her seat and stared out of the back window. A woman staggered out of the shadows. Each step was a struggle, like slogging through mud. Her hair floated in thick tendrils, squirming and weaving around her slender form. The darkness of the night swallowed her features, all but her eyes. They glowed like the eyes of a jack 'o' lantern, burning in the shadows with a brilliant blue light.

Marigold jolted as Louis threw himself back into the car and slammed the door shut. It lurched towards Marigold as it opened its mouth and screamed again. It was louder than before and the car windows rattled, promising to crack as Louis and Marigold cupped their hands over their ears.

"Drive!" Louis commanded over the shriek.

He grabbed the tubs from her lap and hurled them into the back seat. The contents sloshed over the worn leather, but he didn't notice or care. It was agonizing to release her ears. Marigold was sure they were going to start bleeding. But she turned the key and stepped on the gas. The car lurched forward with a hail of dirt and gravel and she swerved to get it back onto the road.

She pushed her foot down to the floor, urging the car faster. The wailing didn't lessen, but cut off within an instant, replaced by a high-pitched ringing in her ears. For a moment she couldn't hear anything else, but eventually, the world came back in patches.

"We need to get back to the boat." Louis was still staring out of the back window, his chest heaving with every breath. "It won't be able to cross the boundary."

"What the hell is it?"

He shook his head, brow furrowed so deeply that if seemed like his skin would break. "It can't be," he repeated in a hushed breath. The car skidded as she took a corner too fast; it fish-tailed and slid over the gravel. Her arms ached as she struggled to keep it on the road. Despite the threat of spiraling out of control, Louis urged her faster. Her heart lurched into her throat as she spotted twin burning lights ahead of them, an unmistakable fiery blue. The light of the high beams barreled closer until they washed over the woman.

"Louis!"

He snapped around, saw the woman, and reached over to grab the steering wheel, keeping it steady.

"Don't stop," he ordered.

They passed the woman in a blur. But the second the woman was out of sight, she reappeared on the rim of light ahead of them. This time, the woman stood closer to the road. And the next time closer still. Then it was in the middle of the lane. She swerved onto the wrong side of the road as they rounded another corner. Mud caught the back wheels and made the car heave again. It took the strength of both Marigold and Louis to keep it from ending up in the swamp.

Ahead of them, the road thinned and the mist thickened. They had reached the thin slip of land they needed to cross to get to the boat. It was barely wide enough for the car to get across. The headlights glistened off the fog and mud. The woman appeared before them, standing in the middle of the road. There was neither time nor room to avoid her and Marigold braced for impact.

The woman released the ear-splitting wail. Marigold winced but kept her eyes open as they collided. The ghost exploded across the windshield like a tidal wave, but the scream didn't stop. Marigold couldn't see through the window. Couldn't hear past the sound. In a rush, the windshield cleared to reveal the side of the paddle boat barreling towards them. She screamed and stomped on the breaks with both feet, yanking the wheel to the side. The tires locked and threw the car into an uncontrollable spiral. The force pulled the air from her lungs and her vision blurred. With a sharp clash of metal, the back of the car slammed into the boat and brought them to an abrupt halt. The seatbelt snapped across Marigold's chest but didn't keep her from smacking against the door. Louis, not having put his seatbelt back on, hit into her other side with a bone-rattling thud.

The mud instantly claimed the car. Swamp water poured in through the fractured glass at Marigold's side as the car tipped. Louis kicked his door open and crawled out as Marigold released her seat belt. She reached up and Louis grabbed her wrists, pulling her up and out of the sinking vehicle.

"Don't make eye contact."

For a second, she didn't know what he meant, but then she caught a glimpse of it. Twin blue lights burning in the back seat. They started running the second her feet hit the ground. It wailed again as they threw themselves onto the rusted surface of the boat, panting and soaked in mud. As the ringing in her ears subsided, she could hear Louis. He kept muttering, over and over, that it wasn't supposed to be here.

"Can you explain now?" she gasped.

"That's a Wailing Woman." He finally sat up and tentatively peeked over the rip of the boat. The woman stood below, a few feet from the gangplank, at the edge of the border that his mother had put into place. Her body quivered like ripples in a tide, but her eyes were unmoving and solid. "What the hell is she doing outside of Mexico?"

***

On hands and knees, Marigold crawled to Louis's side and peeked over the rim. She knew that the Wailing Woman knew they were there. But there was a vast difference between having a ghost know where you are and having to endure being the focus of its dead gaze. The car lights were still on, offering twin beams that cut across the muddy ground. Standing on the edge of the light, the woman watched silently, her limbs unmoving while her hair coiled on unseen currents. This close, Marigold could see water dripping from her greyed and bloating skin. Her eyes glowed like fire, seeing but vacant. Marigold clamped her hands over her ears the second she saw the ghost open her mouth, but it didn't stop the scream from hurting.

"Why isn't she leaving?" Marigold asked after her hearing had recovered. The woman remained in place at her sentry point, neither fading nor drifting, as solid looking as flesh. "She can't get in, can she?"

"I don't think so," he said. With a tired sigh he twisted to sit down on the deck, his back to the ghost. "What the hell is it doing here?"

It was a struggle to keep the agitation from her voice. "Louis, remember how I didn't grow up with this sort of stuff?"

He pulled his hand over his short buzz cut and cast a look over his shoulder. The ghost was still there.

"Like anything else, legends of the Wailing Woman vary, but they have similar key facts. They normally involve a woman that, due to rage, self-pity, or pride, drowns her children when her husband abandons her for a younger woman. She then drowns herself. As punishment, she can only pass into the afterlife with her children, so she's doomed to wander along riverbanks and streams in search of the children she'll never be able to find."

Marigold glanced back at the woman. She had edged a little closer. Light drenched over her features, illuminating her skin even as it passed through her. Real or not, the light glistened off the tears that trickled from her eyes. Even as Marigold studied the pure anguish on the ghost's face, she couldn't summon any great amount of sympathy. She knew first-hand what it was like to have someone hold her under the water and feel her lungs burn for air. She had survived that torture. Her little sister hadn't.

"Seems a fitting punishment," she mumbled.

Louis joined Marigold in studying the ghost. "The problem is, when a strong Wailing Woman gets desperate, they will take anyone they come across. When I was a kid, my grandfather worked a Wailing Woman case. She was strong enough that she drowned a fit, forty-five-year-old man in two inches of water. But I've never heard of one this far north."

"Right," she drowned out the word to make her confusion clear.

"I wish I could give you a set answer, but no one can really explain the phenomenon. It might be the land that creates different kinds of ghosts, maybe different kinds of ghosts naturally gravitate to certain locations, but there seems to be a natural segregation. It's why different cultures have different types of ghosts."

"And Wailing Woman is native to Mexico?"

"Travelling isn't unheard of. Like demons, they can follow certain people. But it's not common." He observed the ghost more closely. She hadn't moved but now trembled with unheard sobs. "Grandpa is going to lose his mind when he hears about this. It's like finding a great white shark in a lake. Would you mind if he came out here and studied her?"

"Well, I can't stand in the way of paranormal research."

Louis stood up and offered her a hand. His smile was weak, as if even a strong breath could destroy it. "She can't break through the barrier. So why don't we at least get cleaned up?"

She hadn't noticed how the swamp water had sunk into her jeans. Algae dripped from her legs and slithered into her shoes. Timidly, she took his hand and let him pull her up. Chills ran along her skin like scurrying spiders. She didn't want to give the ghost her back, but she didn't want to look at it either.

"The boundaries are holding," he assured.

"Right," she said. "So we just have to worry about the ghosts on board."

CHAPTER 5

They had started up the generator, turning the boat into a beacon of light in the mounting darkness. It wasn't a quiet machine and created a constant low hum that competed with the buzz of electricity through aging wires. Louis sat on the deck, enjoying the security of the light while never fully trusting it. They would constantly flicker, but that was to be expected with so many restless spirits around.

Just like the radio stations, mobile reception wasn't fully functional around these parts. He would have to travel at least a mile if he wanted to make a call. The distance seemed longer as the tide began to crawl in. His car would be submerged in a few hours. If they were lucky, the water wouldn't rise high enough to completely flood the engine. But even with that grace he doubted they would be able to get it out of the ditch without a tow truck. And the Wailing Woman was still there, still silently sobbing even as she watched him.

He tapped the phone with quick raps against his thigh. The vision still rolled in his mind. How was the demon strong enough to make a group hallucination? Its access to Marigold had been cut off for months. It shouldn't have been able to do that. Something was very wrong. It made a cold sensation squirm in his stomach and his hands sweat. The woman screamed again and the sound dug into his skull like an ice pick. He closed his eyes and endured it. When he opened them again, he spotted the dubby standing along the water line, a good mile away from the woman. The moonlight glistened off its teeth as it smiled at him and waved. Even as the hair on the back of his neck prickled, he absently lifted his hand and waved back.

***

There were very few cabins still completely intact. There were even fewer that the other passengers had decided she was allowed to use. Two single beds hung from the wall in a bunk-bed-like pattern. They were made out of mahogany wood that was now chipped and beaten. The chains that kept them secured to the wall were layered with rust and she didn't trust them to hold her weight. She used the one on the other side of the wall. It was too thin to be a called a single-bed and sat low to the floor. A moth-eaten curtain dangled from the bed and covered the rest of the distance.

At the end of her bed was a narrow wooden wardrobe that easily held her limited amount of clothes. The hinges were warped, so the door hung at an odd angle. The ghosts didn't bother banging that door, probably because one strong shove and it would break off, so the effect wouldn't be too intimidating. An antique vanity was pressed along the wall between the wardrobe and the bunk beds. A marble sink that had to be rigged to empty into a bottle was between her bed and the door. The place was small enough to light with the glow of one candle.

After all of these months, she had perfected how to bathe in a sink. Time hadn't made it easier to go into bathtubs. If anything, her memories had festered into a full-blown phobia. Sponge baths were effective, but it took far longer to remove the musky odor of the swamp scum. The process and routine made it easier to think about all of the things that threatened to overwhelm her. She had to scrub her foot three times to get rid of the memory of the baby holding her ankle.

She was just putting her long hair up into a ponytail when she heard the laughter. It started with a giggle, as it always did. Like someone trying to keep themselves from making noise and drawing attention. Cheeky, almost playful. Marigold gave her ponytail a sharp pull, having forgotten about the damage to her skull. Pain sliced through her, but she ignored it as she inched towards the cabin door. The laughter steadily got louder. Boisterous and feminine. Marigold reached for the door and slowly closed her fingers around the handle. As quietly as possible, she twisted the knob and cracked the door open.

The laughter snapped into a frantic, manic cackling. It charged down the hall, fast enough to sound like a gale force wind. It burst past her. The force slammed the door open and knocked Marigold off her feet. Her back slammed into the bunk-beds and the air rushed from her lungs in a pained gasp. The laughter continued down the hall and she could hear it descending the staircase to the main deck.

She's going after Louis, Marigold thought before she lurched into the hallway. Her shoulder bumped against the walls in her haste. The metal stairs clattered and shook, and she hurried down them. The laughter never stopped. It grew with malice as Louis screamed. Marigold jumped the last few steps and ran out onto the back deck. It was empty. The outside table and chair had been flipped over. The laughter continued, coming from everywhere at once.

"Louis?"

"Over here!"

She followed the sound of the voice and, in the dim light, spotted Louis's fingertips. They gripped the rim of the deck, the position leaving him dangling over a sharp fall off into the swamp. Marigold dropped onto her knees by his fingers and reached through the gaps in the bars. She latched onto his closest arm with both hands but didn't have the strength to pull him back over. All she could do was hold him stable while he pulled himself up.

The laughter grew louder, an annoying sound that grounded over her nerves. Still, there was no mistaking the slick slosh of something large moving through the water. From her position, she couldn't see what it was. Louis could, and he gripped at the rim with heightened desperation. Her fingers ached as she tightened her grip and heaved back with all of her weight. The rubber soles of his sneakers squeaked across the side of the boat. Their muscles strained. The laughter continued.

Finally, Louis managed to slither his torso through the gap created by the deck and the first rail of the balcony. Marigold released his arm and wrapped her fingers around the top of his pants to help pull him in.

The second he got his footing he flung himself forward and flopped against the floor, panting; one hand searching for her arm and giving her a reassuring and thankful pat.

"I know you have your style, but that would have been a lot easier if you had a belt."

"I'm a suspenders guy," he laughed. It was breathless and far more pleasant than the chuckling that echoed around them.

Marigold inched closer to the railing, careful to keep the bulk of her body safely on board. Flat against the floor, she curled her fingers over the rim and glanced to the water below. The light from the boat combated with the shadows for dominance of the area. In the fray, there was a dozen fiery points of light, each aimed at her. Alligators. She had thought maybe one would have come towards the noise, but not so many.

Are they here because of Mr. Smash Mouth? she wondered. *Do they eat him? What would that do to them?*

"They must have caught the scent of our leftovers," Louis said when she sat back up. He slowed his breathing as the laughter dwindled away.

"They're going to rip up your upholstery."

"Probably," he dismissed. "Do you know what that was about?"

"I call her 'Little Miss Giggles'."

"Really?"

"Don't judge," she said. "It's less scary when they have silly names."

He remained sober. "She wasn't so aggressive when I scouted the place."

"She's gotten more territorial," Marigold said. "But that's what we want right? Something to keep the bad things at bay?"

"We're not going for homicidal. Has she done this to you?"

"She's chased me. Not so much since I've begun staying out of the captain's room."

Louis didn't look appeased. If anything, he looked like he was grinding his teeth against an angry outburst. It wasn't an expression he wore often. He shifted his glare from her into the darkness and

Marigold watched him grimace. She followed his gaze and caught sight of the dubby. It was hard to tell in the darkness, but she was sure it was closer. Her spine shivered as she raised her hand to return its wave.

"How long has he been there?" she asked.

Neither of them had bothered to get to their feet just yet. The chill of the metal seeped through her sweatpants to attack her legs. She had never known the bayou could get this cold. It was the water. It robbed the soft breeze of all of its warmth. Louis hadn't heard her. His eyes were focused on a point on the horizon, glazed over in thought, a frown forever in place. There was something deeply bothering him that he wasn't quite ready to share.

"Louis?"

He snapped out of his reprieve with a slight gasp. "Pardon, Cher?"

"What's wrong?"

"Other than the fact that I was almost fed to some gators?"

"That's not what's bothering you."

Louis smirked. "I'm pretty bothered by it."

Marigold had never had much skill at asserting dominance. The only person who would ever call her stern was her little sister. Jasmine would accuse her of being unfairly bossy any time Marigold insisted that she couldn't have another cookie or run into traffic. But she tried to school her features into something self-possessed and sure.

"Tell me what's going on."

She wasn't delusional enough to believe that her pitiful attempt had any effect on him. Still, Louis heaved a sigh and shook his head.

"It's nothing," he said. "I'm still just surprised. Wailing Woman in New Orleans? But it does look like you're stuck with me for the night. Don't suppose you have a spare cabin."

There was more to it. She could feel it like a pressure in the back of her skull. But for whatever reason, Louis was determined to keep it to himself for now. It would be useless to try and get it out of him before he was ready. While she was stewing over her own disappointment, Louis got to his feet and offered her a hand to help her up. She slipped her hand into his palm and resigned herself to his silence. As if to reassure her, Louis draped his arm over her shoulders and gave her a one-armed hug. She playfully scrunched up her face and shoved him.

"You smell like a swamp."

"That I do. How's your shower situation?"

"I don't know," she shrugged. "I never use it."

He kept his smile, even as a hint of sadness tilted his lips.

CHAPTER 6

There were only two cabins on the boat that had showers. One was the captain's quarters, the other was in the first-class cabin, and they were both pump action. Since the captain's had already been claimed by the swamp and a ghost that obviously didn't like him, he had set up the first-class shower. As it turned out, there wasn't much difference between the shower and a sponge bath. The pump action let him slick up his skin, but the flow dwindled after only a few squirts. It was enough to let him lather up, and he figured that the process would save on their fresh water supply.

The stench of decay still clung to his clothes. They had to be washed. It was lucky for him that, as soon as the weather had turned, Marigold had shown a fondness for oversized t-shirts and sweatpants. It was a preference she had stuck to, much to Cordelia's dismay. It was near impossible to get her into town anymore, so a good portion of her winter wardrobe comprised of his hand-me-downs. At least he would have something to wear while his clothes dried.

Soap suds slid through his fingers as he lathered up his chest. The question lingered in his mind if he had made the right decision. Marigold would resent him for keeping his concerns to himself. He could already see her struggling to accept his silence, but nothing good could come from telling her. He wasn't even sure that there was a problem yet. If the demon had found a way to feed off of her, her fear would only add strength to whatever it was planning.

Small twin lamps bracketed the space where a mirror had once hung. The mirror was gone now, and without its reflection, they struggled to cast any more light than a set of candles. He had left his glasses in the sink, rendering the room into a cluster of formless, fuzzy colors. With his foot, he pumped the lever to get the water to flow. The pipes groaned and rattled within the walls before a weak stream came out of the faucet in sharp bursts.

He gasped as the cold water drenched his skin. The water continued to sputter out and he tried to wipe the remaining droplets of soap from his skin. He flinched at a sudden loud whoosh and a streak of color. Louis blinked into the blurred shapes and shadows. Nothing moved. A slight tremor shook through his fingers and he slowly lifted his hand. Empty space met his fingertips where the see-through plastic of the shower curtain should have been. Releasing his breath with a sigh, he groped along the wall until he found it and pulled it back into place. He turned away. The curtain dragged back against the wall with a thick rasp.

"Stop it," Louis said with as much authority as he could muster. It still came out thick with fatigue and frustration.

He pulled the curtain back into place and held it against the wall. For a moment, there was only silence. Then the back end of the curtain slid across the bar and bunched against his fingers, the tips of the curtain sweeping against his legs. His skin bristled at the touch, his stomach twisted into knots, and a cold lump clogged his throat. He stomped on the pump, determined to hurriedly wash the rest of the suds off and get out of there. The hair on the back of his neck stood on end. He could feel someone watching him. The wall vibrated around the rumbling pumps. He pulled his hand away just as the water spurted free from the pipe. It sloshed over his face and dribbled into his mouth, tainted by the taste of rust.

"Okay, I got it. I'm leaving." He stepped out of the shower and grabbed the nearby towel.

He dragged it over his skin in solid wipes as he crossed the few feet to the sink. The marble basin was cool under his searching fingers. *Where are my glasses?* he thought as his lungs squeezed. He released a slow breath. It churned before him, becoming a misted cloud as the temperature in the room plummeted.

"Old school, huh?" Louis blinked rapidly, vainly trying to clear his vision.

Shadows crowded in around him. Each one moved even as they remained still. He groped at the limited countertop and squinted, but couldn't spot his glasses. Suddenly very aware that he was naked, Louis grabbed for his sweatpants. Forgoing actually drying himself, he pulled his pants on, not bothering to keep the waistband from bunching. He just needed to be covered. The legs of the sweatpants dangled up, but he forced his feet through.

His spine turned to iron as ice-like hands pressed against his stomach. Frigid air ghosted past his ear as a voice, as smooth as molasses yet as gruff as rolling thunder, whispered from the shadows.

"My, my, my."

He jerked away, his feet tripping over each other. The startled movements made his ankle roll and he fell back through the threshold. Moldy carpet ground against his back as he scrambled further from the bathroom. The touch had burnt his skin like dry ice, so he couldn't tell if it was still touching him or if it was just an echoed memory of contact.

The room was darker than the bathroom. The thick shadows made it impossible for him to judge the true extent of each item. His panted breath fogged in front of him, making it even harder to discern anything. Bracing his hands on the floor he pushed himself up, useless eyes focused on the bathroom door. A hand latched around his ankle with an iron grip. It yanked sharply, pulling him a foot over the floor, the jolt knocking his hands out from under him and tumbling him back.

Pressure pushed down on his chest. A solid weight that kept him pinned to the ground. He couldn't move, couldn't breathe, the chill painful against his bare skin. The voice whispered again, so close that he could almost feel the lips against his ear.

"Aren't you a pretty boy?"

Louis craned his neck. Like a captured animal he thrashed against the unseen force holding him, his muscles straining, his back aching. His feet kicked over the floor, colliding painfully with a table. A lamp toppled down and smashed against the ground with a loud crack.

The door to the cabin opened and the specter released him. He pulled himself back over the floor in a panicked slide until his back hit something. With a cry stuck in his throat, he turned around to see a blur of red and white. The face was made of chalky skin and dark, bottomless holes. He jerked away before he heard Marigold's voice.

"What's wrong? Louis?"

"My glasses," Louis stammered. He needed to be able to see. He needed things to be clear. "Can you find my glasses?"

The blur moved around the room, drifting from one side to the other. He watched, his breath slowly becoming invisible as the room steadily regained its warmth. His heart was no longer a painful ache against his ribs as the blur came closer.

"Here, they were on the bed."

"Little on the nose, don't you think?"

"What?" Marigold asked as Louis pulled them on.

The world settled back into place, real and solid, something he could make sense of. Marigold was looking down at him, clearly worried. With a sigh, he shook his head and struggled onto his weak legs.

*****

"You got groped by a ghost?" Marigold asked as she drank her tea. "Can they even do that?"

After the incident, Louis had left the room as quickly as he could. The original plan had been to brew some tea in the kitchen. Only a few pieces of the tea set had survived the crash. They were pretty and delicate and seemed to be fine china. It was a little bit of decadence, and at times, that could go a long way in helping improve her mood. But the ghost there wasn't in any mood for company. It was only skirting things about and drifting cups to the side. Harmless really. But Louis was on edge and his attention darted to every noise. So Marigold had staked what they needed onto a tray and had led him to the small library. It was really just a few leather seats and a cabinet filled with books, but it was small and cozy and easily lit. It was also the one room that the ghosts didn't seem to bother with. The whole time she had called this place home, she had never had an encounter here, and she hoped that the trend would remain for Louis.

"Ghost molestation is a bit more common than you would think." He took his cup with a grateful smile. "It's just never happened to me."

"Are you okay?"

He nodded and leaned into the wing-backed chair. "I feel like I need another shower, but other than that I'm fine."

"I swear if I had known, I would have given you a heads up."

"I don't think you would have known."

"What is that supposed to mean?"

"The way he called me 'boy', what I could sense from him." Louis rubbed his forehead, eyelids drooping. "I don't think you have the coloring or the equipment he's interested in."

"Oh," Marigold said. "Should we be worried? I mean, is he going to leave you alone?"

"I don't know."

"Maybe you should stay in my cabin." Her cheeks heated a little as he turned his gaze onto her. "There's more than one bed. Miss Giggles doesn't get along with the ghost I'm now naming Creeper. They have kind of a turf war going on and some nights they get pretty noisy, but neither of them comes into my room."

"Thanks," Louis gave her a small smile and sipped his tea. "I feel like I just lost a lot of street cred."

"Street cred?" she laughed.

"I stormed a house that not only was on fire but had a demon inside."

"It wasn't on fire when you broke in."

"I think the key thing in that sentence is that there was a demon," he said. "That impressed quite a few people, in the right social circles."

"I bet they'll be quite disillusioned to hear that you were scared by a ghost."

"I didn't have my glasses."

"And that changes things?"

He shrugged. "It does for me."

"How much can you actually see without them?"

"Not much at all." He took another sip, his fingers wrapping more tightly around the small cup. "I have some bad memories of being in situations like that. Never gets any easier."

Marigold really wanted to know what memories were haunting him, but it didn't seem like the time or place to ask.

"You can always focus more on the fact that you were in the shower," she offered. "That would throw anyone off."

"I'd actually prefer to play down that part." His lips twitched into a smile that never fully grew.

He yawned and rubbed a hand over his forehead. When they had first met, he had possessed a constant stream of energy, never tired, never lethargic. Now, each time she saw him, he looked a little more worn. The mounting stress he was under was starting to show, and she hoped that it wasn't because of her. Not because of what she had dragged into his life.

"How is your family?" she asked.

"They're good." He clamped a hand over his mouth as he released a jaw-cracking yawn.

"Business is good?"

"Things are slowing up now that we're out of the tourist season." He looked up to her and realized what she was hinting at. "Are you worried about me, Cher?"

"You just look tired."

"Bad dreams," he said softly.

"Yeah," she said and drank her tea to keep from commenting. She knew about bad dreams. It had been a while since she was able to sleep for more than a few hours at a time.

"It's getting late," he said. "What time do you normally turn in?"

She kept her eyes focused on her cup like it held some great fascination. "I don't sleep at night anymore."

"Cher?"

"I normally go to sleep around dawn," she added with a hint of a real smile. "I feel a lot more comfortable if I can see them coming. Besides, it's too noisy at night."

As if on cue, the low, haunting notes of a cello began to play. The melody was soft, gentle and sweet, coming from everywhere but nowhere at once. They sat and listened for some time, captivated by the sound even as it set her nerves on edge. Louis shuffled in his seat, but she held up a hand to keep him in place.

"Don't bother. I can never find where it's coming from."

"You've looked for it?"

"A few times. I haven't even been able to find a cello. You know," she smiled sheepishly, "the first night I was here alone, I heard it playing. I got it in my head that it wasn't a ghost. That there was some other homeless person wandering the bayous that had turned the boat into their home. I couldn't decide which option scared me more. Ghost or human. Isn't that weird?"

"I've found myself equally afraid of both."

She met his eyes, her humor gone. "You never told me what Delilah did to you. When you were alone with her."

"No reason you need to know, Cher."

It was hard to decide if he actually believed that or if he just didn't want to talk about it. Then again, being locked in a torture chamber with a demon and a murderous sadist couldn't be an easy thing to talk about. She had told him numerous times that she was willing to listen, but he had never taken her up on it. A lifetime amongst ghosts and ghouls hadn't affected him when they had first met. It was hard to shake the feeling that she was the one draining the life out of him. Slowly, precisely, like a ravaging disease that rotted him from the inside out.

The song continued. As sweet as ever but holding a new malice that put her on edge. She hated that song. Louis seemed content to sit and listen, even as his eyelids began to droop. It didn't seem like he was going to last long.

"You look really tired."

He put his tea back on the tray and ran a hand over his head. "It's been a crazy few days."

"You don't have to force yourself to stay up for my sake. Get some rest."

"I'm not quite sure if sleep would be a good idea right now," he admitted.

"Do you want to play a card game?"

He looked up at her even as he rested his head against the wing of the chair. It was as if the music had the opposite effect on him than it did on her. It soothed him, eased him into the deeper throws of his adrenaline crash. He agreed to play a few games but could barely keep his eyes open. The cello got softer, a gentle whisper. Louis's eyes closed as she sorted out the cards. Within a split second, the cello roared back into a concert level, startling Louis awake. He gripped the arms of the chair but couldn't keep himself from drifting off as it lowered again. It lured him and shocked him and did all it could to keep him tittering on the edge of sleep.

Marigold stood up and moved to the bookshelf. She dragged her fingertips along the spines until she found something that could keep her interest. Louis hadn't noticed her departure. His breathing was starting to even out. His limbs grew heavy. Then the cello was just outside the door and he jerked awake once more.

"Sorry, Cher," he mumbled even as he struggled to remember where he was.

"It's okay." She held her selected book in the air and smiled. "Well, I'm going to read in my cabin. If you want to hang out with me, and possibly fall asleep, you're most welcome."

Louis heaved a reluctant sigh but admitted defeat to the demands of his body.

"Okay, Cher." He struggled to his feet and stretched out his spine. "Lead the way."

CHAPTER 7

The feeble light of the single candle was enough to cast a warm glow over the small cabin. The flickered flame released a soft crackle, the tiny noise mixing with the rhythmic sound of Louis's steady breathing. Somewhere, distant within the bowels of the ship, she could hear the lonesome cello. Everything was still, hovering in an easy peace that Marigold knew wouldn't last.

She flicked up from the book she was reading to check on Louis. It was a habit she had honed years ago when her little sister would fall asleep at her side. Jasmine would always insist that she wasn't sleepy, that she could make it through a whole chapter of whatever they were reading together. She would always be asleep before the last page, her beloved Care Bear plush toy cradled in her arms.

Marigold swallowed thickly as guilt twisted painfully in the pit of her gut. She had given Jasmine that toy, Braveheart, the lion Care Bear with a heart on his fat white belly. Jasmine had been terrified of the boogieman and Marigold had told her that Braveheart would keep her safe. She had thought it was just a childish fear, something she would grow out of, something best to dismiss. Now, when the night was quiet and she didn't have anything to keep her thoughts at bay, Marigold was haunted by the thought that Jasmine had known; about their parents, or the demon that they were destined to inherit, or of what was really lurking in the shadows. It was a thought that always broke something in Marigold. When she had learned the truth, Louis had been there for her. There to help, there to believe. He hadn't just given her a stuffed toy and sent her on her way.

Louis was asleep on the lower bunk and for now, the chains were holding. Sleep had claimed him the second his head had hit the pillow, with one foot on the floor and his right arm dangling over the edge. He had kept his glasses on and they had shifted into a weird angle that couldn't be comfortable. She had contemplated removing them but had decided that he would feel better having his sight upon waking. Especially if Mr. Creeper decided to pay another visit. A small smile crept onto her lips as she watched him sleep, chest rising and falling in a peaceful swell.

She had missed this, having someone nearby, sharing her space. Putting her book to the side, Marigold shuffled off of her bed. The flame crackled at her movements and made the shadows shift wildly. As quietly as she could, she slid her feet into her slippers, retrieved the extra blanket at the end of her bed, and approached him. He didn't stir as she delicately placed the soft blanket over him. Bedding had been the one thing she was willing to splurge on. Sleep was not something to be dismissed, a belief that had only gotten stronger after months of forced insomnia.

She reached for her bottle of water and found it empty. Louis had brought a few slabs, but they were all in the kitchen. With everything that had happened, she had forgotten to bring in a few extra bottles to keep in her wardrobe. It was never the best idea to roam the hallways after dark. But now that the thought of getting a drink was in her head, her thirst only built.

It didn't sit well with her to leave the flame. It wasn't unheard of for the ghosts to wander in, and when they did, they normally liked to throw things. But it was hard to take the candle with her and leave Louis in the dark. The night had rattled him. It was obvious even as he refused to talk about it. She couldn't decide what event had broken through his carefully constructed armor, but something had provoked real fear in him. So she resolved to keep the candle with him, after checking and rechecking that there was nothing flammable around it. She'd be quick. Marigold tip-toed to the door and opened it as quietly as she could. The hinges squealed, but she was able to get out without waking up her guest.

The metal walls captured the sound of the phantom cello and carried its melancholy moan through the hallway. In the early evening, the songs were soothing and sweet. Beautiful enough that it had actually nurtured in her an appreciation for classical music. But all that would change after midnight. They were always more energetic in the early hours. She hoped Louis would get enough sleep before they got restless.

The hall lights buzzed and flickered as if they were candles caught in a draft. In what had probably been a decorative choice, the bulbs were encased in lanterns of stained glass. Each one was made of blue, yellow, red, and green triangles that draped the hallway in a cluster of colors and shadows. She didn't like the tricks it played over the peeling wallpaper. Her slippers whispered against the thin carpet and the cold air pushed against her like water as she hurriedly made her way to the kitchen.

The lighting made each hallway look the same as all the others, with shadows gathering at each end. As she moved, the cello song stayed with her, neither getting louder nor softer. It left her with the feeling that she wasn't really moving at all but instead traversing the same hallway again and again. Her insides were squirming by the time she reached the kitchen.

It was in the same condition as they had left it in, with everything scattered over the floor like an obstacle course. It had taken a lot of trial and error, but they had finally found a few places that the ghosts would allow her to store food and water. She had no idea what made these places better than any of the other options, but it wasn't worth the effort to argue. With one hand braced on the countertop, she shifted through the course, taking care not to touch anything, as she made her way to the far side of the counter. The slabs were stacked neatly in a little gap under it, pressed up against the wall. She crouched down, tugged open the plastic wrapper, and grabbed a few bottles to take with her.

With her brow furrowed she stood up. Her breath stuck in her throat and the bottles slipped from her fingers. She didn't feel them hit her feet, didn't notice them rolling to clatter into the items on the floor. Her attention was focused solely on the large toy now sitting in the middle of the counter. It was a toy that didn't exist anymore. It had been destroyed along with everything else when the outraged public had set fire to her family home. Braveheart, Jasmine's Care Bear, sat on the counter, fire-eaten and soaked. Water dripped from its tattered mane and its stuffing poked out in blackened patches.

"Jasmine?" she whispered, even though she knew that the presence she felt wasn't her sister.

It wasn't just the sensation of being watched. Rage and disgust thickened the air until each breath felt like sludge pouring down her throat. Above it all, she could feel its unbridled lust to hurt her. The glee it felt at the very prospect of destroying her in every way. Her stomach clenched under the onslaught and her hands began to shake.

It was a trap. Just like before. The demon was playing on her grief. It knew she longed for something, anything that could tie her back to the life she had. The ignorance she had enjoyed. The last time it had used this trick, it had almost drowned her in a few inches of oil. She didn't want to know what it had planned for her in a room full of sharp objects.

"You can't be in here," Marigold said.

Her voice cracked and her eyes burned as she refused to blink. Not while it was there. Not while it was staring at her through those dead, glossy eyes. She could feel the temperature of the room steadily climb as she refused to look away. The air turned to steam and heat radiated from the metal that lined the walls. Sweat began to bead under her sweater.

Without taking her eyes off of Braveheart, she backed away. The heels of her feet stumbled into the pots that littered the floor, forcing them to the side with a high-pitched scrape. Distance didn't lessen the sensation. If anything, it grew sharper. She was afraid to blink. Afraid of what might change in a split second. The cabinets hit her back as she gasped. Keeping her back to the wall, she edged against the counter, water forgotten. It didn't move. But that scared her all the more.

Attempting to put authority into her voice, she yelled, "Get out!"

The room remained silent and her skin began to burn in the scorching air. She fled into the hallway. Her knees almost buckled at the sudden burst of thin, cool air. The difference left her lightheaded and she grabbed the wall to keep upright. Sweat cooled against her flushed skin, leaving her shivering and dizzy, as the cello began to play once more. She could barely lift her feet as she stumbled down the hallway towards her cabin. There were more charms there, more barriers to keep it out.

It can't hurt you, she told herself, but the words held little comfort. There were many ways to hurt someone without ever touching them. The humming of the lights drove into her skull as the colors shifted in front of her vision. She kept one hand on the wall and pressed the other into her temple. Every hair on her body rose at once and she snapped straight. The sensation of being watched bore into her back. She whirled around, but nothing stirred in the titled shafts of colored light. Even as she stared down the hall, the sensation continued, her primal instincts still telling her that someone was behind her.

The tattered wallpaper was cold as ice as she pressed her back against it. She glanced from one end of the hall to the other. The shadows had grown into inky darkness. From somewhere unseen, she heard the slow creak of a door opening. Her heart hammered, her ears were filled with the sound of her own panted breaths. The wallpaper crackled under her fingertips as she slowly continued her way down the hall. The lights flickered, failing for moments at a time before they came back on with a sickly buzz. Darkness crept closer on both sides.

A scream ripped through the halls, the boat trembling in its wake. Marigold doubled over and clamped her hands over her ears, but it didn't diminish the cry of the Wailing Woman. The electricity surged and the light bulbs tittered on the edge of shattering. Marigold covered her head, protecting herself from the inevitable hail of shattered glass. A single fingertip traced the line of her spine, its searing flesh pressing her skin despite her layers of clothing. She flung herself from the wall and ran into the consuming shadows.

***

Louis was pulled out of the sleeping world with the vague notion that something was pulling over his skin. The gentle candlelight flickered against his closed eyelids and the room remained silent enough to hear the water lapping against the side of the boat. He shivered in the cold, only his feet spared by the blanket that was folded neatly over his feet. He idly thought about pulling it up, but the allure of sleep was too strong. So he just wrapped his arms around himself and rolled onto his side.

Just as he was drifting off again, he noticed a low, scratching sound. It moved in a long glide, and his mind took a moment to identify it. It was the sound of something scraping across the worn carpet of the room. Without opening his eyes, he rubbed his face, groaning when his fingers found his glasses and pushed them into his face before he could abort the movement. He pulled the glasses off and cleaned them on his shirt. Then he heard the scraping rasp again. *Why would Marigold choose now of all times to move furniture?* he thought as he rubbed a hand over his neck. His brain cleared with a snap and he hurriedly pulled his glasses back on, blinking into the dim light.

Ice flooded his veins. Shadows shifted over a chair that now sat in the middle of the room. He recognized it instantly. It was one from the table set on the back deck. The deck that was a few hallways, a staircase, and at least one closed door away. Not willing to blame every occurrence automatically on a ghost, Louis didn't react. Without moving, he shifted his eyes to check if the door was still closed. The chair lurched the second he took his attention off of it. With a grinding scrap, it slid across the floor, charging straight at him.

Louis leaped backwards. He slammed against the wall as the chair screeched to a halt a few inches from the bed. The room quickly fell back into silence, disturbed only by his quickened breath and the crackle of the candle. He swallowed thickly and attempted to calm his heartbeat. The chair didn't react as he reached up and readjusted his smeared glasses.

"Hello." He kept his voice calm, his tone pleasant. In his experience, politeness went a long way to calm agitated people, dead or not. As he kept his eyes on the chair, he used his peripheral vision to check if there was anything else out of place. Other than the chair positioned for whoever sat in it to watch him sleep, everything was how it had been. "Is there anything, in particular, I can help you with?"

A shift of movement caught his attention. He watched as the mattress next to his left thigh began to bow under an unseen weight, the sheets shifting as if someone was sitting down. The hair on the back of his neck rose when he heard someone breathing close to his ear. A new yet familiar sickly feeling settled into him, and he was suddenly pretty sure who his visitor was.

"I know I entered your room without an invitation, and I apologize for that. I assure you it won't happen again," Louis kept his voice gentle but stern. "But this behavior is not acceptable and I would like you to leave."

His skin crawled as a hand of ice rested on his shoulder. For a moment, he was stunned into silence. Mr. Creeper was not an overly strong spirit. Normally, a polite rebuke would be enough to send such an entity like him on its way. Pins and needles rose up over his skin as the hand trailed a path from his shoulder to his wrist. He jerked his arm back and opened his mouth, ready to demand that the spirit leave. That's when a shrill squeak derailed his thoughts.

The sound filled the room. A sharp rusted grind that captured his full attention. He followed the noise to the porthole on the other side of the room. It was set high in the wall and to appease high paying guests, it was larger than on most boats. Large enough for a body to slip through. While a deep crack severed the glass in two, the thick metal frame kept the pieces together. It was kept closed by a thick screw with a flattened end. Beyond the window, the sky was completely black. The sickly feeling in the pit of his gut steadily grew as he watched the screw slowly rotate. The rusted edges shrieked in protest. Despite the ghost sitting next to him, it was the slow turn that made his heart thud.

Under his attention, the screw moved with increasing speed, spiraling out of its lock. That ghastly sound snapped across the room with every rotation. Louis's heartbeat quickened with every screech. Unbidden memories lurked in the corners of his mind, too drenched with childhood fear for him to remember any detail. He couldn't name it, but he knew that he had felt it a thousand times before. The screw continued to spiral until the metal shriek melded into one long scream. The screw toppled from its hold. It hit the floor and he felt the impact in the pit of his stomach. The only sound in the room was the screw rolling over the thin carpet. He flinched when it clicked against one of the chair legs.

Louis's chest heaved, but he couldn't catch his breath. He pressed himself against the wall, eyes locked on the porthole, hands clutching the bed sheets like a scared child. With a long, gasping creak, the porthole swung open an inch. Icy wind rushed inside. The candle flickered at the presence, making the shadows writhe and flail across the walls. Louis swallowed thickly, but it didn't help to calm the hurried pace of his breathing. The cold air wrapped around each of his breaths and churned them into visible clouds before him. For a moment, the room was silent and still.

The night itself leaked through the thin gap. Fingers, as black and slick as a bug's casing, dipped silently into the room. The skin was tight enough that every bone and tendon bulged under the surface. With tips as sharp as a deer's antlers, the knuckled fingers grew over the wall, stretching for inches until the palm emerged. Unbending, the arm continued down until the fingertips brushed against the floor. It was reaching, searching, and Louis couldn't look away. Old fears mixed with the new and turned him to stone.

With a sharp rattle, the chair hurled towards the window. It shattered on impact. The portal snapped shut. The wood splintered and hailed down against the floor. The sudden crash knocked Louis out of his daze and warmth flooded back into his limbs. He could move again and bolted for the door.

CHAPTER 8

Marigold's throat squeezed shut, making her every breath a strained wheeze as she ran down the seemingly endless hallway. The kaleidoscope of colors covered the walls, distorting distance and size. She could still feel it following her no matter how far she ran. Memories of the last time she had been trapped, all alone in the dark with this creature, filled her mind until she couldn't think. Without a care for what was on the other side, she flung herself through the nearest door.

Her heavy breaths echoed back to her as she tried to gauge her surroundings. There were no lights on, leaving the only source of illumination to the mere beams that were able to penetrate the windows. Floodlights had been strung along the sides of the boat, and they gave the thick rolling mist a rusted orange hue. The mirrored wall behind a bar reflected the light, giving just enough to make out that she was in the small cocktail lounge on the third floor. She didn't remember going up a staircase. The cello had once again fallen silent, as if the spirit had fled in the wake of something far worse. She missed the sound of it.

Her fingers trembled as she pressed them against her neck, searching for the thin metal chain of her rosary. She hooked her fingers around it and pulled it out from under her sweater. She held the small metal crucifix tight enough for her palm to ache. The cool metal served as an anchor and helped to steady the rapid pounding of her heart.

A sudden crash made the room quake. The mirror wobbled, distorting her reflection as she edged deeper into the room. The next crash was hard enough that she felt the vibrations tremble through her legs. Another. And another. The tables that remained in the room rumbled with the force. She spun around, trying to determine where it was coming from. It seemed to radiate from everywhere at once. As it sounded again, she finally realized what it was. Footsteps. Something huge was heading towards her.

She squeezed the crucifix tighter as she searched in vain for another exit. All of the windows were too high for her to reach and the only door led straight back to the hallway where the footsteps were coming from. Everything within her screamed for her to find a place to hide, and she couldn't suppress the impulse for long. All of the tables were exposed and the shadows weren't deep enough to hold her. She darted behind the bar and found a line of small cabinets nestled under them. Each booming footstep was louder than the last, drawing closer. The doors rattled, and the few remaining glasses behind her clinked together.

Dropping to her knees, Marigold grabbed one of the cabinet's sliding doors and yanked. Years of grime and dust held it in place. She tugged with both hands as the footsteps made the wood shake within her palms. Another sharp shove and the door inched to the side, just enough that she could slide herself into the darkness beyond. The waterlogged wood splintered under her touch as she squirmed deeper into the cramped space. Stale, musty air filled her lungs as she struggled to get the door closed again. The footsteps stopped in front of the cocktail room's door. She desperately yanked on the cabinet. With a sudden lurch, it slammed shut against her fingers and she bit her lips to keep in her scream.

Huddled in the cramped space she held her breath, straining to hear anything beyond her hiding place. The door opened with a raspy groan. She pulled back, forcing herself into a tight ball, as far away from the slim gap that still remained because of her fingers. Light sliced through the space and fell like a solid bar against the back of the cabinet. The rest was left to thick shadows. She winced as the footsteps came out. With each booming thud, small particles of dust tumbled into the beam of light. She watched them drift to the floor and tried to keep silent. The walls around her shook as the footsteps neared. She clamped a hand over her mouth, unshed tears burning like fire in her eyes.

Alone in the dark, she cursed herself for coming here. She should have gone back to her room, back to Louis. He would have known what to do. The charms could have warded it off. She had given into impulse and now she was trapped in a box smaller than a coffin with the demon only feet away. It would find her. She knew it would. It would always find her.

The shaft of light stuttered as something moved to eclipse the source. Silence followed, weighing on her more than the colossal footsteps had. She could sense it out there, separated from her by only a thin layer of crumbling wood. Squeezing her eyes closed, she waited. Waited for it to find her. Waited for it to strike. Tears shook free from her eyes and she choked on her smothered sobs. Keeping her right hand tight over her mouth, she searched for her crucifix with her left. The metal tinkled softly against the floorboards, sounding as loud as hail in the stillness. She cringed but forced her eyes open. The small slither of light had been completely smothered. Everything was dark. It made her hiding space feel like a grave just waiting to be filled. She could barely breathe through her need to cry.

Water trickled against her hand and for a moment, she thought it was her own tears. But the slick sensation was curling under her, coming up from below instead of trickling down. Her whole body froze as the sensation grew. She could hear it now, water bubbling up and spilling out over the rim of the cabinet. Then the light filled the gap again and she was left staring into familiar eyes. Jasmine's eyes.

Jasmine was crouched down an inch in front of her. The light only touched her face and left the rest shrouded in the shadows. Her skin was grey and slick, water plastered her once golden hair to her head, and eyes met her with an unblinking intensity. Water oozed from her flesh and added to the rancid pool forming underneath them. She smiled, a flash of pearly baby teeth sitting within blackened gums.

Marigold's skin crawled as the thing before her whispered in a sick mockery of her sister's voice, "Found you!"

A scream ripped from Marigold as the rotting creature lunged at her. The world went blank. Hands clawed at her. Her shoulder slammed against the cabinet doors and fingers twisted in her hair, yanking hard enough to tear it from the roots. She couldn't get out. The stench of decomposing flesh churned her stomach. Her lungs burned with the force of her screams.

Panic had taken over her mind, silencing every thought, until all she could do was shriek and squirm and writhe in the pain that snapped over her nerves. Light blinded her and she squeezed her eyes tight against the onslaught. She didn't want to see it again. Not Jasmine. Not like that. The sound of snapping wood cut through her screams. Hands grabbed her and tugged. She thrashed but couldn't shake them off.

"Maggie," Louis's voice hit her ears, making her heart lurch as she fought the urge to gag. "Maggie, it's me."

His Southern drawl eased her need to fight, but she couldn't risk opening her eyes. Not when it could be the demon. Not when it could make her see Louis in the state of decay.

"It's okay, Cher, I've got you." He pulled her close, the solid warmth of his body leaking into her own. She clung to him, hard enough to make him gasp, but still didn't open her eyes. "I'm right here."

***

It had taken a while for Marigold to calm down enough to talk. After that, all she did was insist she didn't want to be here anymore. She wanted to go back to her room. The notion sent tendrils of fear curling through Louis's stomach, but this wasn't the time to tell her so. She needed a safe place. And even if the security the room offered was little more than an illusion, he would let her hold onto it. At least, until morning. Everything could wait until the morning. So together they had begun their journey through the hallways, their process made with the backdrop of the cello's song.

He tried to keep focused on Marigold's story, but it was impossible to keep the reaching hand from his thoughts. He couldn't understand why it had created such a degree of fear within him, why that particular fear had felt so familiar. It bothered him that he didn't know and left fear-like bile in his throat. He pushed the thought aside, angry with his wandering mind. There were other things that needed his attention. In a bid to keep his mind focused, he asked a question.

"The doll, the one on the counter."

"It's a plush toy," Marigold corrected. "And believe me, I remember where I saw it. No need for prompting."

"Did you touch it?"

She looked up at him as they entered the final hallway. "No. Why would I?"

"There are two ways the situation could have played out. Either it was an illusion or it had created a replica. Creating an illusion is like a parlor tick for them. Easy enough. But actually making something corporeal takes a lot of focus and a lot more energy."

"So, it's like a gauge of how strong it is?"

"Essentially."

"Well, next time I'll make sure to poke it."

His shoulders hunched as they neared the cabin door. Not wanting Marigold to see his discomfort, he straightened his shoulders and forced his breathing to slow down. He then discovered that she was too lost in her own thoughts to pay him much attention anyway. Her arms hung limply by her sides and her feet shuffled as if all of her energy had abandoned her. Despite his reservations, he still leaned forward to open the cabin door for her. He might have been scared, but he was also a gentleman.

Sparing a moment to offer him a grateful smile, Marigold took a few steps into the room. Louis followed and swiftly closed the door before he turned and saw what she was looking at. She was standing by the end of her bed, staring at the broken remains of the chair. His stomach lurched when he saw that the window was wide open. Unaware of his discomfort, Marigold knelt down to pick up the screw.

"I'm kind of cold," she said. "Do you mind if I close the window?"

"Please," Louis smiled.

She took a few steps towards the window, and his first instinct was to grab and pull her away. Keeping his eyes on her, Louis tried to appear calm. He busied himself by smoothing down the musty bed sheet of his bunk. It took a few tries to get out the wrinkles that Mr. Creeper had made. He kept a close watch on Marigold as she closed the porthole. The world outside was no longer a bottomless black but had now taken the same off-colored light that matched what could be seen through the other windows. It loosened something within his chest when the pothole clicked back into place. But then she began to turn the screw. He flinched with every slight squeak.

"What happened to the chair?"

Louis straightened but didn't look at her fully. "Pardon?"

She couldn't quite read his expression, so her own hovered between playfulness and suspicion. "What happened to the chair?" she repeated. As if to illustrate the question, she nudged the toe of one slipper against one of the broken chunks. Her brow furrowed. "Is this from the deck?"

Louis straightened his pillows and struggled to keep his tone light. "Mr. Creeper wanted something to sit on as he watched me sleep."

"What is his deal with you?"

"I don't know."

"Are you okay?"

Louis nodded and watched as Marigold wrapped her arms loosely around her stomach. Just when he thought the whole conversation could meet its end, her eyes locked onto him with a spark of suspicion.

"Did he break the chair, or did you?"

"He did."

"Why?"

Louis rubbed the back of his head, letting every ounce of his exhaustion show. "Would you mind if we get into this tomorrow?"

Marigold looked between him and the chair. He could see her

battling with herself to let it go. Eventually, she relented and, with a weary sigh, she crawled onto her bed. Settling back against the headboard, she curled her legs up and hugged a huge, oversized pillow to her chest.

"I'll drop it, I swear, but I just have to ask again. Are you sure you're okay? I might not have dealt with ghost versions, but I've had a few encounters with weird, overly forward guys. You know. If you do want to talk about it."

"He was actually a little less physical this time," Louis said. And having clothes on had helped. "I'm okay, Cher. I promise. I just need some sleep."

"Don't we all," Marigold sighed.

Her whole body seemed to droop as the adrenaline worked its way out of her system. With the pillow cradled carefully in her arms, she rested her chin and stared blankly ahead. In the uneasy silence, Louis sunk down into his bunk.

"Do you think it was really Jasmine?"

She asked the question in a whisper, soft enough that he wasn't quite sure she had wanted him to hear. Anger slithered through him as he watched her hunch her shoulders and squeeze the pillow with the last of her might. In moments like this, she looked small and scared and many years younger than she was.

He had never known Jasmine, and a part of him would always lament that. Through Marigold's stories, however, he had come to know that she had been sweet and kind, and had a stubborn streak that rivalled Marigold's own. Although, since Marigold was her major caregiver, the child hadn't been taught to hide it like her big sister had. He doubted that Marigold even knew that. On some basic level, the two sisters had been very similar.

Louis had also come to believe that Marigold seeing her sister's corpse had hurt her far more than her parents' betrayal. She didn't like to talk about that night, and it didn't feel right to push. But by piecing a thousand little snippets together, Louis had learned that her parents had drowned Jasmine first. That they had left the little body on the bathroom floor when they went to retrieve Marigold. And that she had woken up to see her lifeless sister's body limp against the tiles.

Even if the demon hadn't been present that night, there was no way she would have been able to hide that kind of pain from it for long. It was never a possibility that it wouldn't have used it against her. The longer this went on, the more the demon liked to use her love for Jasmine against her. It gleefully showed Marigold sights she should have never had to see. Planted ideas in her head that would only destroy her as it grew. He wished he could rip it out, but all he could do was watch her mental foundations crack and pray that his kind words could somehow help keep her together.

Louis shifted to sit at her feet. "It wasn't her."

"How can you be sure?"

"I know that, given your experiences, it might seem like only bad things survive death. The rage, the hate, and the sorrow. But the good survive, too. Love survives. If Jasmine came back to you, it wouldn't be to scare you."

He smiled and dipped his head to catch her gaze. Reluctantly, she lifted her eyes to his. There was still a spark of resistance in the bright blue orbs, and he smiled in the face of it.

"What if she's mad at me?" Marigold whispered.

Louis furrowed his brow. "Why would she be?"

She tried for nonchalance and failed miserably. "She trusted me to protect her."

"You couldn't have known."

Marigold nodded but didn't look convinced.

"She loved you, Maggie."

"And how could you know that?"

"I see how much you love her. And children kind of adore everyone."

"Ah, that's almost sweet. I think." Finally, she offered him a real smile. "Are there any happy ghosts?"

"Not many. It's a lot easier for them to pass, to go to wherever we're supposed to go. If they come back, it's normally just for a specific moment, or because they're summoned."

"You can summon ghosts? That's an actual thing?"

"There are ways. None of them are easy," he said.

"What about a Ouija board?"

Louis laughed. "That's not advisable."

"Why?"

"It's like going into an online chat room. There's no way you can be sure who you're really talking to." She sank deeper against her pillows as she listened to him. "You really want to see her again."

"I do."

He thought it over for a moment, picking his words carefully. "A visitation is possible, but they're not common."

Marigold lifted her gaze up to him. "Why does that happen?"

"Sometimes as a warning. Other times they just want to check on their kin."

Marigold was quiet for a moment, watching the candle as it slowly melted the white wax. "Do you think it will ever show me my parents?"

"Probably not until you forgive them. It would hurt more that way."

"I don't think I'll ever forgive them."

Louis sighed. "Maggie, just because they were forced to kill doesn't mean that they were completely void of human emotion. I'm sure they loved you."

"They tried to kill me."

"To protect you."

"I would have preferred they just sat me down and had a heart to heart."

He wasn't quite sure what to say to that, but it didn't seem like she wanted to continue the conversation anyway.

"How long was I out for?" he asked eventually.

She looked at her watch. "I'd say around three hours. If you wanted to try and get more sleep, now's the time to do it. It's only going to get harder later."

"You think I can sleep after all of this?"

There wasn't any hesitation in her reply, "You? Yes."

"You're right," he said with a smile.

His stomach twisted a little at the thought of sleep, but he wasn't in the position to let the opportunity slide. Marigold watched him carefully for a moment. In a bid to ease her worry, he smiled and went to stand. She grabbed his wrist.

"I know I sound like I'm five, but would you mind keeping close?"

He almost sagged with relief. "Of course, Cher."

Louis wasn't quite sure if she had picked up on his apprehension, or if he had just gotten lucky, but for whatever reason, Marigold shuffled over to the side of the bed by the wall. He glanced at the window, just to make sure the screw was still in place, and settled back down against the bed. The solid weight of his glasses felt weird as they slid down on his face, but he didn't remove them. Marigold's bed was a lot more comfortable than the bunk. The pillow-topped mattress welcomed him and cradled him like a cloud, and the sheets were soft cotton. He had given her a few protection washes, concoctions of bless oils designed to keep her sleeping area a little safer, and everything smelt like ginger and spices. He had always liked the scents and it soothed some of his raw nerves. Shifting his glasses into a more comfortable position, he closed his eyes and tried to let sleep come. The old, uncertain fear still lingered, even as he tried to push the thoughts of the arm from his mind. But it refused to leave him. There was something he was missing and, even as he mulled over the mystery, he wasn't certain he wanted to know the answer.

"I'm sorry I left you alone," Marigold whispered.

He opened one eye and looked over to her. She was still sitting up, but her grip on the pillow had loosened.

"No reason to be sorry, Cher."

"Mr. Creeper hasn't bothered me before. Maybe if I had stuck around, he wouldn't have come in. It didn't even occur to me."

"He gave me a shock. Nothing more. No need to dwell on it."

He let his eyes drift closed once more and took in a deep breath. The candle was burning low but still emitted a comforting light. Slowly, tension began to leak from him and his mind started to drift. Then he heard a gentle tapping, like someone hesitatingly trying to get his attention. Blinking past his sleep, he turned to look at Marigold.

"What do you need, Cher?"

"That wasn't me."

Her words were cautious and hesitant. It grabbed his attention and made him look up.

"Do you know who did?"

She shook her head. The tapping came again. A few short raps and then silence. This time, it was easier to pinpoint where they were coming from, and Louis squirmed at the discovery. They had to be at least ten feet off the ground, but someone was tapping against the glass of the porthole. The mist rolled in, constantly changing patterns, slow and undisturbed. Shadows existed everywhere within the off-colored fog, but nothing moved. As they watched, the tapping came again, the source unseen.

"Has this ever happened before?" Louis asked. It hadn't occurred to him earlier that this could have been a night event that she had kept to herself.

"No," she whispered. "I'm not really looking forward to any more surprises tonight."

Again, the soft tapping like knuckles on glass filled the room. A quick set and then silence. Marigold turned to Louis and he forced a smile. Without a word, they came to the decision to ignore it. They both settled back, trying to reassume their previous ease. When the knock came again, they silently shuffled closer to each other.

CHAPTER 9

The design etched into the headboard dug painfully against her spine, and it had been at least half an hour since her leg had fallen asleep. But she refused to move. Despite the sharp, random rapping against the glass, everything had once again been lured into a slumbering calm. She knew that the peace didn't depend on her, and that it was hardly likely to be shattered if she shifted her position, but she wasn't willing to tempt it. So she remained still, enduring the throb in her back and the tingles in her leg, listening to the steady flow of Louis's breathing. It seemed that no matter what he was exposed to, sleep never eluded him. She envied him for that.

It wasn't her first night spent in the grip of insomnia, self-imposed or otherwise, and for a while, she managed to entertain herself with her book. But eventually, her mind began to wander from the words on the page. Afraid of what it might decide to bring to the forethought of her thoughts, Marigold delicately reached into the pocket of Louis's jacket and pulled out his mobile phone. She had never been all that captivated by the games he had on it, but insomnia made just about anything interesting. Not wanting to disturb him, she muted the sound and brought up a game where all she had to do was match bright and oddly happy rocks.

But it turned out that without the sound, it couldn't hold her interest for long and eventually, she was forced to search for something else to keep her eyes open. She moved into the saved files and found the folder of spirit photography Louis had gathered. Louis had taken each picture that filled the extensive file. Some he had gathered while helping people like Marigold, those stuck in positions they didn't know how to escape. Others he had quickly snapped while he was leading ghost tours around the streets of New Orleans. She didn't understand why he got so excited over most of them. The only abnormalities looked more like spots of dust that had caught the light at the right moment, or like something shiny had reflected the flash to create a lens flare. It didn't matter how many times he enthusiastically explained why they were significant, they still just looked like dirt. But there were others. The ghosts in those pictures ran the spectrum of looking like human-shaped fog to those you would mistake for a living person. Finally, she came to a series of pictures featuring the Wailing Woman.

She knew he would have clicked off a few photographs while she was cleaning up. He wouldn't have been able to resist. Every time he saw something strange, he just had to take a picture of it, or study it, or document it in some way. It was almost a compulsion. Before they had brought her here, she had spent some time in his apartment. He had dozens of boxes filled to the brim with photographs and testimonials, voice recordings and copies of antique documents. The sheer volume of what he had gathered was enough to make any non-believer question their convictions.

Tap. Tap. Tap.

Marigold didn't know which ghostly figure had decided to adopt this new tactic, but they were completely unreliable. She had timed the knocking for a while but hadn't been able to find a pattern in times or the number of raps. It was just random. A quick knock on the window glass and then silence, as if it just wanted to remind her that it was there. She did her best to ignore it and focused her attention once more on the little screen.

Swiping from one photograph to the next, she allowed herself to fully study the woman. She was twisted and frail. Pitiful, really. But she couldn't bring herself to feel the amount of sympathy for her that she was sure Louis held. If anything, Marigold thought the woman had skipped out on the punishment she deserved.

She lifted her thumb to swipe to the next photograph when something stilled her finger. Unable to pinpoint what had grabbed her attention, Marigold lifted the phone closer to her face and peered at the photograph. The niggling feeling continued; something she couldn't quite place but couldn't dismiss either, as she studied every inch. The camera flash had highlighted the trees that surrounded the ghost and the mud that remained untouched under its feet. The ghost itself was void of color, only shades of black and grey that left her looking like a photonegative. All but her eyes. Her eyes glowed blue.

Louis jerked in his sleep. The sudden movement made her flinch, and she swallowed down a startled yelp. Barely keeping her hold on the phone, Marigold rubbed a hand over her face and stinging eyes. It wasn't likely she would make it until dawn. It had surprised her to learn that she had a set limit of adrenaline she could tap into. That fear alone wasn't enough to keep her awake. Not indefinitely. Eventually, her brain would shut down and take what it needed, preservation instincts be damned. But knowing this didn't make it any easier to give in. To the vulnerability. To the dreams. She shook her head, drew in a sharp breath, and searched for something to keep her attention.

Louis released a pained whine but didn't move again. Even as his face scrunched up and twitched, his limbs remained flat against the mattress. His breathing came in short gasps and were punctuated by fractured moans. Whatever he was dreaming, it wasn't good. She reached out to grab his shoulder but didn't make contact. Nightmares were a necessary evil here. If she woke him now, he would just be dragged into another one the next time he slept. *Is it worth it to wake him? If I did, would the next one just be worse?*

She was still trying to decide when the tapping came again. Sharp and quick. Shock froze her. That hadn't been on the window glass. It had been on metal. Not knowing whether to be confused or scared, Marigold turned to face the porthole. It was still latched firmly in place. She couldn't see anything beyond it, but then she never could. The resounding silence played tricks on her sleep-deprived mind. She found herself questioning if she had heard it correctly. If she was just mistaken and it had been the same as any other. That it hadn't moved. But she knew what she had heard. The knocking had come on metal, but she couldn't remember where on the ship it had resonated from.

Surrounded by silence, her hand poised over Louis's sleeping form, Marigold waited. The minutes dragged by but she couldn't bring herself to move. She just waited, her eyes trailing the room as if she could pinpoint where the sound had come from by sight. Even though she had been waiting for it, she still jumped at the short series of taps. She flattened herself against the bed, eyes focused on the ceiling. The tapping had come from inside the boat, from the floor above her, right above the bed. A shiver ran down her spine. She didn't dare move. Even as her rational mind told her repeatedly that having a ghost on board wasn't anything new, her insides wouldn't listen. This felt different. It felt like an intrusion. A violation.

Still unwilling to get up, to take her eyes off of the ceiling, she shuffled closer to Louis. Their shoulders pressed together and his solid presence helped ease the twist in her gut. Ease, but not release.

Tap. Tap. Tap.

The sound came from directly above her. It echoed along the metal like ripples rolling out across a lake. She grabbed Louis's wrist with more force than she had meant to. He whined under the pressure but didn't open his eyes. She wanted to shake him. Wanted him to be awake with her now, to hear what she was hearing, if not to make it stop then to have him tell her she wasn't insane.

Her insides twisted and squirmed. Something was watching her, like a snake preparing to strike, and she squirmed under the fixed attention. Louis flinched beside her. Swallowing thickly, Marigold focused on her breathing. She felt the air travel down her throat. Felt her lungs expand and relax. In and out. She let the world filter down to that one sensation and felt her heartbeat begin to slow. Tension eased out of her shoulders. Her heart fought for calmness, then imploded when she heard the tapping again. It wasn't above her anymore. It wasn't on metal. The sound had come from the foot of her bed.

***

Louis couldn't move. It was as if he had been encased in concrete and could barely force his lungs to take more than a desperate gasp. Struggling not to panic, he quickly took in the room. Marigold's cabin stood around him, the same as it ever was and yet different. Cold and dark. The candle had burnt itself out, leaving the room to the mercy of the foggy orange glow. He struggled to get up, but a weight against his chest kept him pinned in place.

Then came the tapping. Soft and quick, rattled against the wood at the end of the bed. He couldn't lift his head. The muscles of his eyes strained as he tried to catch sight of what was down there, what was hidden in the gloom. A barely audible cackled sound rose over his panted breaths. It was a high-pitched, demented sound that drove him to panic. He thrashed and struggled, but his body held as firm as stone.

As graceful as a spider rearing up to strike, long pitch-black fingers fanned out from behind his feet. The bony digits, void of any joints, folded over his shoes. He felt the pressure of the touch, and his gasped breaths became broken whines. Without a sound, the creature rose up into view. Its skin was a thin sheet that molded to bones and tendons, leaving it as a bulging, misshapen skull. He watched Louis with eyes of polished silver that reflected the orange light and dark shadow. It rose higher still and the sharp lines of its cheekbones almost severed its head in two. Louis tried to scream as it peeled back its leathery lips, exposing rows of erratic fangs in a mangled smile.

It looked down at him with that mocking, victorious grin, and Louis knew that this was the creature that had reached in through the porthole. The same fear as before thrilled him, driving him to hyperventilation as his jaw refused to open, his head spinning with the lack of oxygen. It moved as smoothly as a snake uncoiling, rising up to loom over him. Despite its brittle form, its body blocked out the light like a goliath. Its shadow fell over Louis, cold and oppressing, forcing the last traces of air out of his lungs. Without taking a step, it drew closer, its smile still in place, the silver discs of its unseeing eyes fixed on him with startling intensity.

Louis struggled against the unseen force that held him down. It didn't matter. His body wasn't his own anymore. This thing had taken it from him. Had claimed him. It hovered closer until its grotesque face filled Louis's vision. The smile widened. Its breath fell over him with the putrid stench of spoiled blood. Louis screamed, but his jaw was locked in place, muffling the noise into a pathetic mewl. Louis squeezed his eyes shut against the sight. The pain in his chest grew. He was sure that his ribs couldn't take much more. That they would crack under the pressure. Its twisted hands latched onto his chin, pushing it up, forcing Louis to expose his neck. Louis's eyes rolled and his body trembled with the force. He couldn't see it, but he knew it had opened its jaws, and he waited for the strike of fangs.

CHAPTER 10

The bed shook as Louis bolted upright, a blood-curdling scream ripping out of his throat. Marigold had never heard someone scream like that. It made her heart stutter and her mind go blank. He thrashed and kicked, eyes wide but unseeing, and she scrambled to the other side of the bed to escape his flailing limbs. Every time she tried to get closer, he whirled on her, forcing her to dodge away from his frantic shoves. She had to scream to be heard under his panicked cries. She told him it was okay, that it had just been a dream, but it was of no comfort. No matter what she said, he just continued to fight his unseen attacker. He toppled over the edge of the bed and landed hard on the floor. The jolt seemingly bringing him back to himself. Chest heaving, he looked around the room, his movements jerking as he tried to see everywhere at once.

Marigold gripped the edge of the bed as she cautiously shuffled closer. "Louis?"

He didn't respond, didn't even look at her. But he had stopped screaming and she was grateful for that. Still gulping down each breath, he patted his hand against his jacket pocket. The slight movement grew into sharp slaps when he didn't find what he was looking for. At first, Marigold didn't understand and tried to speak to him again, but then it clicked and she snatched up his mobile. Cradling it in the palm of her hand, she presented it to him. It was hard to reach out and keep her distance at the same time, but his eyes flicked to the small device and he lurched forward. Before she could move, he grabbed the phone from her hand and ran for the door.

She called after him, her voice rising with mirrored panic, but he didn't hesitate as he disappeared across the threshold. Her feet tangled in the bed sheets as she sprang up to follow him. Yanking her feet free she hurried out into the hall just in time to see him turn a corner. As she ran after him, she wished that she had spared a moment to put her slippers on. The thin carpet didn't offer any protection from the cold metal underneath. Louis didn't wait for her. He barreled down the hallway, making a beeline for the door that opened onto the balcony. The mist poured into the boat when he wrenched the door open. It was so thick that, after only a few steps, she lost sight of him completely.

"Louis!"

Her fingers dug into the wood of the doorframe as she paused at the threshold. The mist rolled over her, cool and slick against her bare skin. It seeped into the carpet underneath her feet and numbed her toes. The floodlights were still on, working with the fog to completely hide the world behind a swirling golden haze. She squinted harder, unable to even distinguish the railing that she knew stood only a few feet in front of her.

The crack in her voice set her on edge, "Louis!"

She could hear him, the pounding of his feet as he raced over the metal, but was unable to tell which direction it was coming from. The wood dug into her palms as she struggled to decide which way to turn. His footsteps faded, replaced by the lapping of water and the gentle, breathy howl of the wind passing through Spanish moss that hung from the nearby trees. Swallowing thickly, she slowly edged one foot out onto the deck. The fog had left a thin layer of water on the floor, and she almost pulled back at its frigid touch. She bit her lips and took another step, leaving one hand on the doorframe like a lifeline.

"Louis, where are you?"

His silence kept her clenched on the doorframe until her knuckles turned white. There was a sudden flash of light and she spun towards it, some strands of her red hair catching on the moisture the fog had left upon her cheek. Holding her breath, she waited for anything else to stir. Another flash. She abandoned the door and broke into a run. A part of her mind screamed at her that she had no idea what she was running towards, but her need to find Louis was greater. She pressed on, one hand held high to keep herself from colliding into anything.

The damp metal froze her feet and the airborne droplets of water collected in her hair. Each moist breath carried the chill deep into her lungs. She peered into the fog, still unable to discern anything out of the gleaming haze. The cloud before her flashed again. Marigold pushed herself faster, ignoring the way her hair rose on the back of her neck. The fog held tightly to its secrets. Tightly enough that she didn't see the massive shadow until it was almost upon her. She gasped and threw herself to the side. Her hip struck the railing, and her own momentum almost toppled her over. She latched onto it, still holding on even after she had regained her footing. It couldn't have been Louis. The shadow had been too fast. Too quiet. Marigold glanced behind her, back to the doorway she had just abandoned. It was impossible to see it anymore. She longed to go back. Instead, she lifted her hand once more and continued walking into the abyss.

The soles of her feet squelched against the balcony with every step and her heavy breaths churned the fog. The cold prickled against her fingertips and robbed them of their sensitivity. But still, she pressed on towards where she had seen the flash of light. Something surged through the water, a quick splash of something large, and she flinched before she could stop herself.

"Louis." Despite her conviction, her voice came out in a broken stammer.

The name choked off as a shadow began to form before her, too shrouded in the mist for her to be able to judge its true size or shape. The air tingled against her outstretched hand, and she suddenly felt vulnerable, exposed. She slowly pulled her hand back towards her chest, not wanting to draw the attention of the darkening shadow. But it wasn't darkening, she realized, it was coming closer. Marigold shifted her weight, torn between surging forward and fleeing back to the relative safety of her room. On the hope that it was Louis, she called for him again. There was no response. The figure loomed closer.

Hesitantly, she took a step back, her feet squishing into a small puddle of water. The figure followed her in complete silence.

She pressed her hand against her chest like a shield, forcing her wrist into her sternum until both bones ground together. The figure drew closer and she gave into the urge to run. She didn't hear it follow, but she felt it there, right behind her, closing in on her. No matter what she did, she couldn't increase the distance between them. Her feet hammered against the floor. The slick shine of water on the balcony threatened to trip her with every step. She couldn't see anything beyond the fog. It consumed everything and left her blind. The figure loomed close behind her back, almost close enough to touch. She could feel it. Picture it perfectly like a photograph plastered across her eyes. It was right there. A hand grabbed her arm and yanked her violently to the side.

She didn't have time to struggle and her feet interlaced. The hand pulled her through the doorway and back into the multi-colored hallway. Pain sliced up her arms as she attempted to break her fall. The carpet ripped and grounded against her forearms as she slid to a stop. Behind her, the heavy metal door slammed shut with a resounding crash. She flipped over, but the hand grabbed her again, tight enough to bruise, and hurled her to her feet.

The fear in the pit of her stomach eased when she looked up to see that it was Louis pulling her along. She stopped struggling and tried to get her legs to work, to fall into step beside him. He didn't say a word as he pulled her into a breakneck sprint. The hallway was barely wide enough for them to run side by side, but he kept her close as they barreled the short distance back to their cabin. Behind them, the hull door slammed open, unleashing the fog into the boat. Marigold glanced over her shoulder to see the mist churning in like a dam had broken.

With his crisp shirts and suspenders, Louis didn't advertise himself as a man of strength. His generally mild manner gave Marigold the illusion that she would be able to overpower him. So, she wasn't prepared for him to wrap an arm around her waist and practically throw her into the cabin. She hit the bed hard enough to force the air out of her lungs. Before she could get up, Louis slammed the door closed and slid the lock into place. He mumbled, the words coming too fast and low for her to understand any of it, and hung his gris-gris on the door handle. With that done, he ran to the window and ensured the lock was in place.

"Louis?" Marigold asked. She didn't dare get up. Didn't want to get in his way. "What's going on? What happened to you?"

He didn't pay any attention to her as he continued to bless the room. Fear slithered in her gut like a horde of snakes. Anything that could provoke this level of terror in Louis was something worthy of being scared of. She glanced around the room but couldn't find what had riled him up. She wanted to help but could only ball her hands in the sheets and wait.

"Louis, what is going on?"

Without a word, he tossed her his phone. It hit the blanket by her knee and she hurried to pick it up. After hitting in the code, the screen lit up, already in the photo application. She clicked onto the album to see the last photographs he had taken. Her mouth opened as she looked over each one in turn. The fog had stolen the finer details of the pictures, but some things were still distinguishable. The side of the ship, a porthole, and a figure of pure black. Its skin shone in the flash. The spindly, bony creature possessed elongated limbs and fingers that looked more like extended knives. It was clawing at the wall. Clawing to get in.

"What is it?"

Louis finished what he was doing and seemed at a loss for what to do next. After a moment of hesitation, he ran over to the bunk and began yanking the pillows free of the pillowcases.

"That's a mare," he said, his voice frantic as he rushed back to the porthole.

He tugged and tucked the pillowcases around the glass until it was impossible for them to see out, or for anyone to see in.

"I know this one." She kept her tone as light as she could, hoping that it might somehow calm him down. "It's where the term 'nightmare' originated from, right? It sits on your chest as you sleep and gives you bad dreams. Is that what happened? Did the mare come for you?"

His new task was complete, leaving him with nothing to help focus his restless energy on. He paced the small space, his whole body jolting with unspent adrenaline. Eventually, he dropped down on the end of the bed, but he couldn't keep still, couldn't keep from checking over his shoulder as if he expected the mare to suddenly appear behind him. After one final glance, he sunk down onto the floor. He hunched his shoulders, ducked his head, and slouched down as if he wanted to hide. Marigold looked from the porthole to the door and slid down next to him. She knelt as close as she thought he would let her, seeking comfort within the shared space. Her stomach was a chunk of ice that she couldn't dislodge, and it grew with every second that he refused to meet her eyes. Finally, just when she thought she wouldn't be able to take his avoidance anymore, he looked over to her.

"Why are you so scared of a mare? You told me they were common. And generally harmless."

"It's not what it is that scares me," Louis whispered. "It's *who* it is."

He pointed to the phone as if the picture contained all the answers. She flicked through a few more photographs before she found the one he must have been thinking of. It was a close-up of its twisted and mangled face. Her gut twisted as she looked at it, but something deep in her mind told her that there was something familiar about its features.

"That's John La Roux." The fear in his tone made her shiver. "The Vampire of New Orleans."

***

Louis pulled his glasses off and pressed his hands against his eyes. He couldn't get his heartbeat to slow down, couldn't stop his mind from repeating what had just happened. Marigold was next to him, her hand poised over his arm but never making contact. He was scaring her, he knew he was, but he couldn't shake off the overwhelming, consuming dread that had settled within him.

He let his head drop back to rest against the bed and tried to steady himself. But the position stretched out his neck, reducing it to an exposed strip of flesh. He snapped his head back up. Marigold kept making soft broken noises, like she started a dozen sentences at once but couldn't see any of them through to the end. He couldn't leave her stranded like that. Needing a sense of normality, he cleaned his glasses on his shirt. He licked his lips, took care to position his glasses perfectly back onto his face, and opened his eyes.

Marigold was staring at him. It looked like it physically pained her to keep all of her questions contained behind her pinched mouth. Still, it only took a second for her to notice that he had shifted his gaze onto her. He offered her a shy smile and was rewarded by a weak one in return.

"I'm sorry, Cher. I didn't mean to give you a fright."

Marigold shuffled off of her knees to sit on the floor. "I'm going to need you to explain this." She held up his phone, thankfully with the back of it facing him. He really didn't want to see that again. At his silence, she continued, "You told me mares couldn't hurt you, not really. Not physically."

"They can if they have something to feed off of."

"What do you mean?"

He shook his head and tried to sort out the facts that she would need to know from the jumble of information within his skull. "Ghosts can be parasites. They can establish connections to things like places and objects, and use it to strengthen themselves."

Marigold was quiet, and he was hoping that she wouldn't latch onto what he had left unsaid. That bit of hope shattered when she held his gaze and asked.

"Can it latch onto a person?"

"Yes."

She nodded solemnly. "You think it's latched onto me?"

"I think it wants to. It's why it's so desperate to get in."

"I think it was," she said. "I heard tapping. It was coming from inside the room."

Louis took her hand and gave it a quick squeeze, as much to reassure himself as her. "I was asleep. It can always come through the barriers using a sleeping person. We have no control over that, not right now."

"If I fall asleep, will it be able to latch onto me?"

Louis shrugged. "It's not an exact science, Cher. I just want to know why it's here."

Marigold tried to keep her tone light, but it came out strained, "Maybe he's just checking on his kin."

Guilt lingered clearly in her blue eyes. It was hard to look at. "What I mean is I want to know why he's on this plane of existence at all. How he had even become a mare. There's something I'm not getting and that makes me nervous."

"Louis," she began in her 'no nonsense' tone. It was always hard to keep from smiling when he heard it. "I know you think that I'm not strong enough to take the truth, and maybe you're right. But I don't have a choice. I have a demon on my doorstep and ghosts as my roommates. Ignorance isn't going to help me. You can't shield me from these things."

"I'm not trying to."

Her sudden burst of laughter startled him. "You are a horrible liar."

"Maybe I'm trying to shield you a little," he said as he rubbed the back of his neck. "I just don't want you to worry about things you don't have to."

"I saw how you reacted, Louis," she swept her hand out. He wasn't sure how she thought the gesture captured the situation. "It's pretty obvious that this is something I need to worry about."

"This wasn't about a mare, Maggie. Not entirely."

"Then what was it about?"

"It's about him."

"Who?" Her brow furrowed. "John?"

He tried to hide the way he flinched at the name. He was sure he didn't accomplish the feat. Staring down at his hands, he hunched his shoulders against the cold feeling creeping into his chest.

"One of the best and worst things about growing up in my family was that I always knew there were things lurking in the dark. I knew there was evil in the world. I knew that monsters were real. And I knew that some of them wanted to hurt me." Fears that he had buried long ago bubbled to the surface, as strong as they had ever been. "John La Roux was my boogieman. He was the one I checked under my bed for. I even nailed my window shut, refusing to open it even during summer. I was convinced that one day he would come crawling through it."

People went on ghost tours to learn about the macabre and the levels of depravity humans are capable of. And nothing was quite as twistedly bazar as the La Roux family. Each generation was comprised of serial killers and madmen. He had extensive files on the history of her family, or at least what information had been made public knowledge. When this had first begun, Marigold had been determined to face all the monsters lurking in her family tree. He had given her the files but had no way of knowing just how much she had managed to stomach. For some unknown reason, out of all the carnage and horror the La Roux line had unleashed onto the world, the crimes of John La Roux had stuck with him the most. It might have been because, when he had first heard of him, Louis had been a prime example of his victim of choice. He hadn't yet turned thirteen, his room was on the ground floor, and his window hadn't been visible from the street.

Finally deciding to place her hand on his forearm, Marigold spoke softly, easing him back out of his thoughts. "John died in the 1930's."

"And it really seems to have slowed him down," the words came out with a sharper edge than he had intended. He cleared his throat and tried again. "Do you remember why they called him the Vampire of New

Orleans?"

She hesitated at each word, watching him carefully. "He would break into children's bedrooms and kidnap them. After he drained their blood, he would come back. He'd—" she flinched, "he'd tuck his victims back into their beds for their parents to find."

Louis could feel the weight of his fears, both old and new, bearing down on him.

"When I was little," he eventually began, "I had honestly believed that John La Roux would kill me. Not that he could, but that he *would*. Like it was destined to happen."

"And yet you're still helping me?"

He glanced over to her and smiled. "Of course."

Marigold shifted closer, shuffling until their thighs pressed together tightly. Looping her arm around his, she hesitantly threaded their fingers together. Her skin was cold and he squeezed her tightly, both in reassurance and to coax some heat back into her flesh. With a sigh, she rested her head on his shoulder.

"You're a good man, Louis Dupont."

He smiled. "And you're a good woman... A good woman who completely mangles French names."

Vibrations rattled against his shoulder as she laughed. She didn't lift her head as she squeezed his hand and lightly slapped him with the other.

CHAPTER 11

Neither of them attempted to move as the hours passed and the boat slowly came alive around them. The new energy that coursed through the boat was enough to keep Marigold's drooping eyelids from falling entirely. Idly, she thought that it must have been past midnight because it seemed that the spirits had taken to their normal, disturbing, routine. It was hard to hear the once prominent sound of the cello over the malicious, crazed laughter that roamed the halls at random. There was a constant pounding noise, like the beating of a hollow drum, and under all of it, Marigold caught the slight crash of the pots and pans being hurled around the kitchen. Louis didn't comment on any of it. If it wasn't for the slight flinch he gave at every sudden crash, she would have thought he didn't even hear it.

The candle had burnt low and released its wax in a milky pool over the floorboards. She watched it, thinking she should light another one. But she didn't want to get up. Sitting on the floor had grown steadily more uncomfortable, and the draft that crept under the door made her shiver, but she was busy reveling in human contact. It was always uncertain when she might next be able to have an opportunity to feed her tactical nature. As much as Louis meant to her, they didn't really have a relationship where she felt comfortable asking for a hug. Louis never flinched away, but he rarely initiated. Only when she really needed it. It was nice to have a moment where she could just pretend that life was normal.

Louis abruptly straightened, the movement catching her off guard. Her stomach sank as he looked over his shoulder to the still blocked window.

"Did you hear that?" he whispered.

She was just about to respond when he lifted a hand to silence her. Then she heard it. It lingered under the ruckus that consumed the boat, echoing from somewhere far off in the bayou. A horrified, short scream. A woman's scream.

"It's a trick, right?" she asked. "They're just trying to lure us out."

He met her gaze, his hazel orbs void of the conviction she had been hoping to find. Before he could answer, they heard the scream again. It was moving closer at a rapid speed. Marigold cringed at the raw terror of the sound. In unison, they got to their feet and inched closer to the porthole. They both stood within arm's reach of the pillowcases, but neither made an attempt to remove them.

"Twenty bucks says that when I take this off, John's face is plastered against the glass," Louis struggled to joke.

She didn't find it funny but appreciated the effort. "I'm not taking that bet."

Focusing his eyes onto the porthole he timidly reached up, his fingertips brushing over the material but not taking hold. Marigold moved closer to his side, not knowing if she was trying to gain comfort or supply some. They stood like that, waiting for something unknown, frozen in place. But when the scream came again, far closer than it had been before, Louis grabbed the pillowcases and yanked. The thin material ripped in places as it revealed the porthole. The fog pressed close to the glass, hiding the rest of the world and leaving nothing but an orange glow.

Their eyes met again. She had expected something to try and get in, and now that it wasn't, Marigold didn't know what she should do. Louis's Adam's apple bobbed as he swallowed thickly. He edged closer to the glass. The horrified scream sliced through the night, drawing him forward to peer through the glass. A second later, he backed away, eyes wide and mouth hanging open. He was already moving to the door when he called over his shoulder.

"Stay here."

"Like hell," she snapped as she instantly started to follow him.

With one hand on the door, he glared at her like a scolding parent.

"Sorry," she smiled. "Like heck."

"Maggie—"

"You're running headfirst into a trap. I'm coming with you."

"It's not a trap."

The cry of the Wailing Woman made her flinch, her hands instantly going to her ears. Louis took the moment of distraction to wrench open the door and once more run into the hallway. She wasn't going to let him leave her behind again and kept close on his heels. Her ears were ringing as they ran through the colored halls, past the scattered object tossed from the kitchen, and further to the back of the boat. When sound finally returned, she could hear the grinding roar of a car engine.

"Go back to the room," Louis said.

"Weird stuff happens when we split up," she shot back. "Splitting up isn't safe."

They burst out into the night and the fog instantly enveloped them. Apparently, Louis had accepted that she wasn't leaving him because he reached back and took her hand, keeping her close as they made their way to where the gangplank was supposed to be. They tripped over bottles and ropes and other odd items before they found the opening in the railing. In the distance, the mist brightened in the wake of the car's unseen headlights. The cry came again and Louis's grip tightened to the point of pain.

Only about a foot separated them, but she still wasn't able to make him out clearly. She searched for his features but only found smudged shadows. His anxiety was clear in his voice when he bellowed his cousin's name into the fog.

"Cordelia!" His fingers tightened when the only response was the drone of the engine and the shriek of straining breaks.

"Are you sure it's her?" Marigold asked.

"Positive."

Breaks screeched in the mud, metal collided with metal, and the boat shook with the force. It seemed like Cordelia had fallen to the same fate they had when the Wailing Woman had forced them off the road. Louis lunged for the gangplank, but Marigold held tight and threw her weight back until he stopped.

"I have to help her!" he snapped.

"What help will you be if you get lost in the mist?" She held his hand tightly as she dragged him to the side. After a moment of blind groping, her movements made frantic by the woman's screams, Marigold finally found the coil of coarse rope she had tripped over. She pressed it against his palm to make sure he knew what it was. "Help me tie this around my waist and I'll go down."

"What? No! I'll go."

"I'm not strong enough to pull you up if something goes wrong," she said.

Cordelia's next scream came from the side of the boat and was met with the sound of metal and thrashing water. Even in the dim light, Marigold saw Louis tense up, torn between his need to protect his family and his will to keep Marigold safe. But the sheer desperation in the cry broke his resolve. With quick and easy movements, Louis wrapped the end of the rope around Marigold's waist and knotted it tight. She rocked with the jolts as he tugged sharply to check his work.

"Anything happens, tug on the rope and I'll pull you up." He then rushed to the edge of the boat and yelled into the mist, "Cordelia, stay out of the water!"

Not wanting to give him a chance to change his mind, Marigold ran past him and down the gangplank. The wood and metal rocked with her every step. It wasn't until the frosty mud swallowed her feet that it occurred to her what she had done. Her bravado crumbled and she was left frozen in place, taking in her surroundings. Behind her, the floodlights were bright discs upon the fog, but in front there was nothing. Just a steady progression into darkness. She couldn't hear the engine anymore. Or the screaming. Only a slight murmuring over the normal sounds of the bayou.

She ran her fingers over the coarse material of the rope, assuring herself that it was still there, and headed to the right. It was odd to hope that Cordelia had crashed in the same area Marigold had, but she hadn't. Marigold wasn't sure she would be able to find her. The incoming tide had loosened the mud and made her struggle for any progress. Mud oozed through her toes and claimed her feet, holding onto them with a sucking sensation. She could hear things slithering through the muck, unidentifiable in the mist.

"Cordelia!" Her lungs strained as they fought to keep her from making a sound. Her instinct was to be quiet. As if her body didn't want to admit that the ghosts already knew she was there. That even though she couldn't see them, there was no doubt that they saw her. She swallowed thickly and tried again, this time able to summon more strength. "Cordelia!"

A scream ripped through the air and she broke into a hobbled run towards it. Shadows began to emerge from the mist, details only coming as she closed the distance. There was a truck, tilted on its side, half of it sunken into the mud that surrounded the boat. A shadow loomed by the front door, hunching through the window and moving in sharp jolts. Cordelia's terrified cries came from inside the truck and Marigold launched herself forward without thought. Shock rattled through her when she struck the shadow and found herself making contact. The shadow was as solid as flesh.

She couldn't move fast enough to miss the blow. Between the fist colliding with her jaw and the mud clutching her feet, Marigold collapsed against the sodden earth. Pain exploded behind her eyeballs and her head spun. Breathing hard, she looked up and managed to focus on the shape in front of her. The mist cleared enough so that she could see that the shadow was a man. His narrow but strong back faced her, and after the single strike, he didn't seem to bother with her again. His attention was solely focused on trying to pull something out from the truck. The whole time, he worked a constantly babbled string of muttered gibberish.

As the pain ebbed from her skull, she realized he wasn't mindlessly rambling. His tone made it clear that, despite his fear, he was trying to reassure someone who she couldn't see. Agitation had sped up his words and his thick Cajun accent made it near impossible for Marigold to understand him. She struggled to her feet and he whirled on her with a snarl.

"You move and I'll hit you again."

Cordelia cried out from the truck, her voice reduced to a garbled, bubbling noise. With that, he completely lost interest in Marigold and threw his torso back through the window. He hunched up like a feral cat when Marigold rushed over.

"I'm Louis's friend. Let me help."

"I can't get her out. Something's got her."

He shifted enough to give Marigold enough room to see. The dim lights of the dashboard cast a slight glow over the inside of the truck, allowing her to make out a few things within the mist that clogged the air. Water was quickly filling up the truck, sloshing up over the form of a struggling woman. Out of the murky depths of the swamp water, Marigold could see a figure shifting under the surface. It had a firm hold on Cordelia's foot and held her in place as the water rose. The man had both her hands but he couldn't break the hold of the creature in the water. The struggle pulled Cordelia taut.

Marigold struggled with the knot of the rope, tugging and thrashing until she could unwind it. It was a simple plan. Crawl in, get the rope around Cordelia and get Louis to join the struggle. She hurriedly explained as the man held tightly to Cordelia, his force of will the only thing keeping Cordelia's head above the rising water. As the words tumbled out, she realized just how much she wanted him to argue. But he didn't. He just nodded, his attention never leaving Cordelia.

While the man was tall, his shoulders were narrow, so he didn't have to move too much for Marigold to slip through the remaining space of the window, bracing her feet on the dash and the windshield to keep her out of the water. Cordelia's strained position made it easier for

Marigold to wind the rope around her exposed torso. But the water made the rope float and bunch as Marigold tried to get it into place. The water sloshed over her arms and her heart hammered each time she had to push her hand into the inky liquid.

Marigold's feet slipped and she dropped into the icy, slime covered water. Cordelia looked at her with wide eyes but didn't say a word as Marigold struggled to find her footing. Her movements became wild as she tied the rope into place around Cordelia's chest.

"Okay," Marigold said as something slipped past her leg.

The man tugged sharply on the rope and an instant later, it pulled taut. Marigold gasped in pain as the rope coiled around her arm and bit into her skin. She had somehow tethered herself to Cordelia. The rope tightened and she clenched her teeth to keep in a scream. She pulled back and the moss on top of the water stirred and opened. She saw a shadowy figure. She saw a pair of glowing blue eyes. A second later, Cordelia was yanked down with a colossal strength. Both women struggled vainly to keep inside the truck. The force pulled harder and they were both dragged deeper into the frigid bayou.

CHAPTER 12

Louis slid across the deck, the rusted metal tearing the back of his shirt, as he refused to release his hold on the retreating rope. The pull twisted him around until his side slammed against the railing. The coarse material of the rope burned his hands as he desperately tightened his grip. He lurched up with the pull until he was able to set his shoulders and slam his body back down. His arms strained and his fingers began to bleed where the rope rubbed them raw, but he couldn't stop the constant drag. Out of the mist, he heard a voice. Fear distorted the words until he couldn't find any meaning in them but he bellowed in response all the same.

"Grab the line!"

The rope snapped taut, as tight as a bow string, making the metal railing release a musical ping as the rope struck it. Louis shifted to brace his feet against the railing, tightened his hold, and threw his weight back. He couldn't gain an inch.

"I can't see them!" the voice called back.

Louis pulled again but couldn't get it to move. He needed something larger. Something heavy.

"Get up here," he called. "Help me find the anchor!"

Moments later, the gangplank screamed as Cordelia's new husband emerged from the mist. Rene glanced around, blinking into the shroud, completely disregarding Louis in his search for the anchor. Without a word, he ran into the mist, leaving Louis to continue his struggle with the rope. Suddenly, the rope turned slack and he slammed down against the deck with a solid thud. He scrambled to get back up, his hands snatching one over the other to take full advantage of the moment of reprieve. A few feet of wet rope passed through his hands before it pulled taut again, making him fight to maintain the progress he had made.

They're still underwater, his mind screamed at him. *How long have they been under water?*

"Get down."

Rene's warning barely gave Louis enough time to flatten himself against the deck before he heard the anchor hit the water on the far side of the boat. The rope zipped against the railing as the anchor plunged into the bayou. Water sprayed over him as the rope dragged past, following the anchor and hopefully bringing the girls closer to the surface. With another resounding ping, this louder than the last, the rope pulled tight, vibrating an inch above him. Louis rolled to the side and thundered down the gangplank, Rene already at his heels, urging him faster. Rene pushed in front and they bolted towards the truck. From somewhere deep in the shadows, they could hear the sound of something thrashing. They could only hope it was the girls.

***

Marigold sucked in a deep breath the second she broke the surface. Water sloshed into her mouth and a few traces of moss made her gag, but oxygen still hit her lungs with a dizzying rush. She yanked, feeling her skin peel as she struggled to free her arm. Cordelia grabbed the window frame with both hands, holding on tight to keep both of their heads above the water as Marigold worked. Twin pinpricks of blue burned under the water as the Wailing Woman rose from the impossible depths, her twisted fingers reaching up to grab them once more. Pain sparked on Marigold's arm as she contorted her wrist until it came close to the point of breaking. She wrenched her arm down and, with a final rip of skin, her hand slipped from the tangles of the rope. Cordelia heaved her torso out of the open window. Water sloshed over Marigold, striking her head and making her sputter as she shoved at Cordelia. Finally, she managed to slither out of the window and

Marigold was able to grab the door frame to follow.

The process would have been easier if Marigold braced her feet on the dashboard and chair, but she couldn't bring herself to be still for too long. The eyes still glowed in the darkness, and she was sure that at any moment a bony hand would wrap around her ankle and drag her back under. Her wet fingers skidded over the metal and she tumbled back into the water. She could see the Woman, floating just below the door, her hands only inches from Marigold's feet. Hands reached in from above and latched onto her shirt, hauling her through the gap and into the night air. The whole time Marigold never looked away from the Woman. The ghost made no attempt to follow but merely watched as Marigold was dragged away.

Marigold's feet had barely touched the mud before the hands on her forced her into a sprint. The haunting screech of the Woman drove painfully into her ears and shadows streaked through the fog. The flashes of darkness upon the tainted fog swirled around the group like debris caught in a hurricane. Her heart pounded against ribs that felt too small to contain them, her lungs strained to function while water still lingered within them, and each step turned the muscles of her legs to fire. The cool metal of the gangplank was a welcomed relief. It rattled in time to her throbbing wrist as they threw themselves up the short distance, almost tripping over their own feet as their legs struggled to meet the demands of their mind. Each one of them fell onto the deck, heaving and panting, and too scared to turn around.

Marigold dropped onto all fours, water dripping from her hair as it fell in sludge-covered curtains around her. A shrill whine filled her ears as she wretched, heaving up mouthfuls of water even as she tried to catch her breath. As the sound faded, the mumbled words of the people around her came into focus. Her head felt like a cement block. Her neck protested its lift. After a few aborted attempts, she managed to lift her gaze to the people around her. Cordelia and the man clutched at each other, whispering words of comfort and reassurance. The sight made it click in Marigold's mind that the man with her was Rene, Cordelia's new husband.

Marigold had never seen either of them before and it was oddly surreal to see them now, here, soaked, mud-stained and shaking from fear and dispersed adrenaline. Blinking her vision clear, Marigold tried to get a closer look at Cordelia. From what she could tell in the muted light, Cordelia and Louis shared a strong family resemblance. They both had the same dark skin, full lips, and pointed chins. However, it appeared that Cordelia's wide eyes were quite a few shades darker than Louis's. Even now, Cordelia carried with her a refined beauty that terror couldn't rob her of; an inherited grace that couldn't be taken away.

In contrast, Rene was gruff and chiseled. He looked to be forged by struggles and hardships, and was more than a little bitter about it. There were scars on his knuckles and a sharp glint in his narrow gaze. Each time he shoved his light brown hair out of his eyes, the fringe would tumble back into place. Before Marigold could see any more, Louis shot to his feet. His hands twisted in their clothes as he forced the couple to their feet and pushed them towards the door to the boat. Marigold scrambled up and followed. He slammed the door shut the second after she slipped through. The short burst of activity had robbed them of what little strength they had gathered, and each slid down to sit on the floor. Time stretched out in silence, no one really knowing what to say as their breathing returned to normal. Rene was the first one to speak.

"What the hell just happened?" he growled.

Louis was too focused on reassuring himself that his cousin was unharmed to answer, so Rene's glare focused on Marigold instead. It struck her that she had never had to explain any of this to another person. She had always been the one who needed the rules of her new nightmarish world explained to her. It was humbling and intimidating to be on the other side of things, and she didn't quite know where to start. But surely, having just married a Dupont, a family with deep and numerous ties to the paranormal, he would be aware of the basics. So, what exactly was he asking? His glare narrowed at her hesitation and she stammered out an answer.

"That was a Wailing Woman."

"What?" Even utter confusion couldn't rid him of his permanent scowl.

"A ghost."

Rene stared at her for a moment before he snarled. "Ghosts don't exist, so that ain't likely."

Cordelia blindly reached out and draped her hand over his forearm, the small diamond of her wedding ring glistening even in the dim light.

"I've told you that they do, sugar. More than once."

"Oh, for sure," his thick accent curled around every syllable. "But I ain't crazy, so I never believed you."

Laughter sputtered out of Louis despite his attempts to keep it in. "Well, tonight is going to be interesting for you then. Very educational."

"This ain't no time for joking. That bitch ran us off the road, she almost killed us, and she trashed my truck!"

Caught up in his anger, Rene switched from English to French. The change didn't slow him down but instead allowed him to rattle off words at a greater speed. Louis and Cordelia both took to the shift easily, but Marigold was left unable to follow the rest of the conversation. No one seemed to notice or care that Marigold had been removed from the equation, and she was suddenly aware of the distance that separated her from the others. Cordelia was nestled between Louis and Rene, close enough to feel the warmth from both. Marigold was by the door, with nothing but aged carpet and cold steal within her reach. She itched to cross the distance, to join the safety of the pack, but she wasn't sure if it would be welcomed. So, she remained where she was and tried to fend off the growing chill of her soaked clothes by wrapping her arms around herself.

Eventually, the foreign words drifted into silence. It was a little startling to once again be thrust into the dynamics of the conversation when they all turned their attention to her. She swallowed and tried to smile, repressing the urge to wave when they continued to expectantly stare at her.

"I'm sorry, I didn't understand anything any of you have said in the last five minutes."

Cordelia straightened her spine as a delicate smile curled her lips.

"You must be Marigold," she said. "I'm so glad to finally meet you."

"Hi," Marigold replied, only realizing after it was down that she had, in fact, given an awkward wave.

"Well, don't you look just like Louis described!"

Marigold's brow furrowed with confusion. *So, basically a pale redhead covered in freckles,* she just managed to stop herself from saying aloud.

"Not to be rude," Louis cut in, "but why are you here? Aren't you supposed to be on your honeymoon?"

"We were," Rene scowled.

The tension that coiled in Rene's shoulders left him as Cordelia once again placed a hand upon his arm, this time cupping his bicep.

"This might shock you, Louie, but when you don't show up where you're supposed to be, people in your life start to worry. Your mama called us in a tizzy and asked us to come out here to check on you."

Rene's smile was too tight to show teeth. "Basically, we're here because you can't work out how to use a cell phone."

Louis and Cordelia fixed him with matching glares. In that moment they looked enough alike to be twins.

"There's no cell reception out here," Louis said. "And you've met the reason why I didn't go for a walk."

Cordelia perked up. "Since we're back on the topic. Why have you not mentioned that Poppy La Roux is hanging around?"

Marigold snapped her eyes to Louis to find him watching her with the same questioning expression. She shook her head slightly. She had no idea what Cordelia was talking about.

"Who the hell is Poppy La Roux?" Rene asked.

"A woman who lived in the 1930's. She ran an orphanage for

unwanted children or children that couldn't be calmed in polite society," Louis explained. "Poppy would promise to raise the children for a monthly fee. However, she would kill the infants and continue to collect the payments."

"She killed babies?" Rene's words dripped with disgust. He shook his head. "I'm still confused. You saw this Poppy woman when we were outside? Like her grave?"

Cordelia hid her emotions well enough that it was hard to tell if she was annoyed or merely frustrated when she answered, "She was the one trying to drag me into the water."

Rene blinked, licked his lips, and seemed to take care in how he framed his next question. "A woman from the 1930's was in the water and strong enough to drag you down?"

"She also ran us off the road and made that god-awful noise that I'm pretty sure left me with permanent hearing loss," Cordelia said.

Marigold finally found her voice again and asked, "Are you sure it was Poppy?"

"I'm sure."

When Marigold searched for Louis's eyes again, he wasn't looking at her. Instead, he gazed across the floor as he struggled to make sense of what he was hearing.

"Is that possible?" Marigold asked. "None of the children she killed were hers."

"It's not impossible. They were still her charges, but I've never heard of it before," Louis mumbled to himself. "And even if she did become one, I can't imagine she could have haunted these waterways for so long without anyone noticing. Why now? Why here?"

"So, it might not be her?" Marigold pressed.

"The woman was three inches from my face," Cordelia cut in. "I know it was her."

"Apart from the fact that ghosts aren't real."

With an edge of frustration, Cordelia turned to her husband. "Sugar, I'll be ready to believe whatever you want, as soon as you can provide me with a 'rational' explanation as to what happened out there." She raised her eyebrows expectantly and stared as Rene opened and closed his mouth a few times. Despite his efforts, he didn't make a single sound. "Well, now that we have that cleared up," she turned to Louis and finished, "that woman out there is the late and despicable Poppy La Roux."

"Why not?" Louis ran a hand over his head. "We have John La Roux banging on the door as a mare, why not Poppy as a Wailing Woman?"

Cordelia's mouth opened. "I'm sorry, repeat that?"

Louis's hands twitched as he lifted his head and tried to smile. "Oh, that? Yes, well, John La Roux is a mare. The boundaries are holding for now, but he looked rather persistent."

"Louie," Cordelia said carefully, "how are you faring with that? I remember a few issues you had when you were little."

"I'm dealing," Louis cut in quickly. He shook his head like he was trying to jumble all of his thoughts around into something he liked more. "So, we obviously have a problem that I can't solve."

"I don't know about any of that." Cordelia shivered and leaned into Rene's side. "All I know is that Poppy La Roux just tried to kill me and there are a lot of corpses in that water."

Marigold's skin went cold as her eyes widened. She held her breath, hoping that Louis would let the comment slide. But his eyes were a fire against her cheek, and she could feel his anger seeping into the air.

"Could you say that again?"

"Well, the water was murky and dark," Cordelia said hesitantly, continuing when Rene wrapped a protective arm around her shoulders. "But I'm sure I saw some bodies in there. The gators and critters had gotten at them, but they all looked alike. They had all been related."

"Or identical?" Louis asked, his eyes never leaving Marigold.

"Maybe. I didn't get that close of a look."

"Did you touch one?"

"Not on purpose, I can assure you. But it touched me."

"And it was solid?"

Cordelia's mouth twisted. "As much as rotting flesh can be."

The room fell silent. Marigold's lungs were burning from keeping in the breath she couldn't bring herself to let go. She inched her eyes towards Louis, but quickly looked elsewhere when she saw the barely contained indignation written across his features.

"What haven't you told me, Marigold?" he said.

"It didn't seem like something to bother you with."

"Marigold."

"And I kind of told you," she said softly. "Remember? Every day, at the same time, one of the ghosts does his thing."

"And 'this thing' was becoming corporeal?" Louis snapped. "No, you did not tell me that."

"Does it really matter?" Marigold said.

"Yes."

"Why?"

"Because no ghost on this boat has enough energy to do that," his voice continued to grow. She had never heard him yell before and she cringed under the onslaught. "For any of them to even get near that kind of activity, they would need to latch onto a powerful energy source."

"Isn't that a good thing?" Marigold said. "They're keeping the things out there, well, out there. Don't we want them to be stronger?"

"The boundaries aren't built to handle something like that."

Marigold finally met his gaze. "What?"

"Think of the boundary spells like battlement walls. They're designed to withstand attacks, but there are limits. Having damage being inflicting on both sides of the wall isn't helpful. It's the exact opposite of helpful." He froze for a moment, the fire draining from his face as his eyes widened.

"Louie?" Cordelia asked. "What is it?"

"The demon's feeding them," he muttered. "That's why the ghost can become corporeal, and Miss Giggles can physically move me, and Mr. Creeper can touch me."

"Who?" Rene asked.

Louis ignored the question as he continued, "It's feeding them, making them stronger so they wear down the boundaries on this end. Poppy and John didn't become these ghosts on their own. It had probably latched onto them in the past and refused to take its claws out, even in death. Somehow, it brought them from the other side, all to put strain on the boundaries. They weren't designed to withstand this kind of attack."

"It can't do that. It wouldn't have the strength. Not after you cut off its access to Marigold," Cordelia was quick to say.

"I don't think it was drawing its strength from Marigold," Louis said. "It has someone else. Someone or something with a powerful spiritual energy."

Marigold felt a shiver down her spine. "What about the dubby?"

Louis's head snapped up and he scrambled to his feet. "We've got a big problem."

CHAPTER 13

"Are you actually telling me we're in danger?" Rene snapped. "What the hell is wrong with you people?"

Louis was at the porthole, squinting into the shadows, trying and failing to catch sight of the dubby. Cordelia moved to stand by Louis, craning her neck to join the search but having as much luck as her cousin.

"Sugar," Cordelia said. "I love you and I need you to be calm for me."

"Calm? You're talking about being under siege by the ghosts of murderers, who are taking orders from a demon, and you want me to be calm?"

Cordelia turned to face him, a patient smile on her lips. "Here are the cliff notes. There is a demon out there that wants in. Nothing good would come of that. Louis and I are looking into it and will let you know if and when it's time to worry."

"Why does it want in so bad?"

"That's my fault," Marigold said. "It wants me."

Rene looked at her for a long moment before he shook his head and muttered, "Bloody La Roux."

"It's not her fault," Louis was quick to say.

Suddenly, a thousand voices joined to create a howling scream that ripped past the sides of the boat. They all threw themselves back from the windows, eyes wide and mouths agape. The screaming continued, growing shrill and blazing, as if the gates of hell had opened within the mist.

"What is that?" Rene asked.

Louis's eyes trailed over the ceiling, his jaw hanging loose. "That's the boundaries fracturing."

"We have to get out of here," Cordelia said. "Louis, we can't stay."

"And we can't go," Louis replied. "Not while they're out there. Poppy will try to drown you again."

Cordelia was quick to answer. "But she might not want us to actually die. She had a chance to pull Marigold under the water again, but she didn't."

Louis's eyes snapped to his cousin. "They want us trapped here?"

"Why? If they want her dead, why not just kill her?" Rene spared Marigold a glance. "No offense."

"Poppy is Maggie's relative," Cordelia said. "If she's only here because the demon is forcing her, maybe she doesn't really want to hurt her kin. Maybe she's trying to let her live."

"Or the demon wants me alive to breed me." Marigold said it in barely more than a whisper, but it commanded everyone's attention. "That's what Aunt Delilah was going to do. The demon needs a La Roux. I'm the last one."

"Your family is seven kinds of crazy," Rene said as he came closer to Cordelia. "Okay, so I gather that them getting in is bad, so there ain't no use in spit-balling about why it will be bad. Let's talk damage control."

"Damage control?" Louis repeated.

"Just because they get in here doesn't mean they have to get us," Rene said. "What do we do?"

All eyes fell onto Louis and he tried his best not to notice. Still, he begun to pace, frantically rubbing the back of his head with both hands. Cordelia perked up as an idea occurred to her.

"If the boundaries can't take the strain, why don't we release the tension?"

"Good," Rene said. "How?"

"We release the ghosts on board. Send them over to the next life."

The words had barely passed her lips when laughter rolled down the hallways and slammed into Cordelia with brute force. Thrown off of her feet, she smacked against the nearest wall. She released a yelp on impact and tumbled down onto the ground. Rene was next to her instantly. His fingers gently probed and prodded, checking her for any broken bones. The laughter dissipated as Cordelia braced a hand against Rene's knee for support.

"I'm okay," she groaned as Rene continued to check the back of her head. "I'm okay."

The walls rattled and the floor swayed as something struck the hull of the boat. Rene pulled Cordelia to her feet. She was still weak kneed, and he wrapped an arm around her waist to take most of her weight. The pounding continued, each making the room vibrate. Marigold looked to Louis, her stomach clenching when she found a look of bafflement etched onto his features. His eyes darted around the room, never stopping on any spot for more than a few seconds.

"We need to get out of here," he mumbled.

"That's what I've been saying," Rene snapped.

The conversation was brought to a halt when the thumping suddenly stopped. The world was swallowed by silence. It hovered over them, pressing down until their ears rang with it. No one moved. The desire to speak, to somehow break the tension that twisted her up, gnawed at Marigold. She could almost feel the words at the base of her throat but she couldn't force out the slightest sound.

Something slammed against the door, hard enough to make it jolt on its hinges. It remained closed but rattled. They staggered back from the thunderous knocking. After three booming raps, the unbearable silence returned. A heartbeat later, Louis darted forward and grabbed both Rene and Marigold by their shirt sleeves. Wordlessly, he tugged, urging them further back into the boat.

They fell into place behind him and fled into the hallway. The colored shafts of light, now darker than they had been before, swayed and twisted in no clear pattern. The constant shifting made it impossible to tell the true width or depth of the hallway. The walls seemed to swell and recede like the ship had become a colossal beast that breathed around them.

Louis ran straight for Marigold's cabin. He flung open the door but didn't enter. Instead, he stood to the side to hurry the others in. Before they could get near, a hand reached through the open doorway, latched onto his shirt, and yanked him into the room. The door slammed shut on its own, muffling Louis's screams. Rene caught up a second later. He rattled the door handle and slammed his fist against the wood, but couldn't force it open.

Cordelia and Marigold joined his assault on the door, the three of them were forced to squeeze together tightly to fit into the small space of the threshold. The sound of cracking wood and groaning metal joined Louis's pained cries. Still, the door held firm. Rene pushed the girls aside, clearing the space so he could throw his body weight against the door. But the hallway was thin and didn't allow enough room for a run-up. Each time his shoulder collided with the door, there was barely any force behind the blow.

The door wouldn't budge and it wasn't going to. Marigold stood back, helplessly watching until a thought hit her. She turned on her heel and ran for the kitchen, ignoring Cordelia's cries for her to come back. Terror dripped from every syllable Cordelia spoke and Marigold couldn't bring herself to reply. If she heard the same fear mirrored in her own words, she might not be able to get what they needed.

It didn't take long to get back to the kitchen. The bawling, screaming wind of the failing boundaries had begun to blow again. Stronger this time. It shook the boat in violent heaves, forcing Marigold off her feet. She staggered, her shoulder bouncing off of the doorframe to the kitchen, and she gripped it tight to steady herself.

The kitchen no longer stood in organized chaos. Nor was it just the normal selection of pots and pans that were being whipped into the spirit's frenzy. Everything that wasn't bolted to the floor now hurled around the room like leaves caught in a swirling whirlpool. They clattered against the walls and rebounded off the floor, the impacts only driving them into a faster, wilder pace.

Still catching her breath, Marigold tipped her head to get a better look at the room. Instantly, the items barreled towards her. She threw herself back, pressing against the floor and covering her head with both hands. Items whipped out of the doorway and ploughed against the wall with bone crushing strength. China shattered and pots slipped like cracked nuts. She lowered one arm just enough to see what she had come for was now embedded within the wall. A meat cleaver. It was rusted, but still solid enough to inflict some damage and might just be able to hack through the thin door. Her hands itched to reach out and grab it, but she knew that the second she did, the ghost would send another array of items towards her.

Marigold pushed up onto her feet, stabilizing herself by pressing her fingertips against the floor like a sprinter at the starters block. Louis's screams and the frantic cries of the others spurred her on. She lunged across the space. Something metal and flat smacked against her thigh. Pain exploded along her side as she slumped against the ground, sliding just far enough to be behind the protection of the wall. Sitting up, she crawled a little further, just enough to ensure that she was completely out of the way. Only then did she allow herself to release the sharp cry that she had kept behind clenched teeth. It felt like her leg was in a vice and each pulse of her blood only added to the pressure.

Still, she forced herself up onto her good knee and checked to see how much closer she was to the meat cleaver now. It was within reach, and she would be able to keep most of her body protected by the wall, but not all. She would have to reach into the open space of the doorway. Her back would be completely exposed while she struggled to pull it free. With quick sweeps, she searched the area for something that could offer any amount of cover. There was a discarded pot lid, by no means large enough to shelter all of her, but big enough to keep her head protected. Steadying herself, she listened to the chaos of the ghost within the kitchen. *What if it has more knives?* The second the thought came to her, she lunged forward, needing to move before she lost her nerve. She snatched up the pot lid and employed it as a makeshift shield as she reached for the cleaver. The wood was solid and cool against her palm and while she could wiggle it, the wall refused to release the blade.

Items drove into the pot lid with too much strength for her to keep the metal from colliding into her head. A few strikes and it felt like her skull was about to crack. Her vision blurred and her head throbbed, but she refused to let go of the cleaver. An object struck her shoulder like the blow from a baseball bat, and she couldn't contain the scream. She reeled back, still holding the cleaver. The wall shattered as the blade tore free and she flopped onto her back behind the safety of the wall. Tears welled in her eyes and pain clogged her throat. Marigold wanted to stay there. To just lay still until the pain ebbed away, but Louis was still screaming. She forced herself to get up, to cross the threshold once more and head back to the cabin.

Each step brought a new spasm of pain. It flickered through her thigh and reduced her run into a broken hobble. She limped down the hallway, holding the cleaver high for Cordelia to run over and take it from her.

"We don't have an axe," she winced.

Cordelia ran the short distance back to Rene and handed it over. With a hand on her stomach, he urged her back a few more steps, clearing the space before he attacked the door. He channeled every ounce of his strength into each swing, his muscles bunching as they forced the blade into the thin wood. The meat cleaver dug in easily, gouging out large chucks with each blow. Cordelia kept as close as she dared and called to Louis through the gap Rene was creating. Louis begged them to help, for them to hurry, and the sheer fear in his words broke Marigold. The tears she had been holding back dripped from her eyes as she helplessly watched Rene gouge open the door.

The wood gave way with a sickening crack and Rene pushed himself inside. Before he had fully stepped through, he froze, his body rigid and jaw slack. Cordelia and Marigold rushed forward and pushed the stunned man aside in their haste to pull Louis free. The room was a disaster area. There wasn't a single item that had faced the ghost's brutality and remained intact. Debris littered the floor and the bunks dangled as loose chunks of wood against the wall. Louis was pinned against the far wall, struggling against unseen hands that held him a few feet above the floor. They dragged him up over the dented surface until his head brushed against the ceiling. He thrashed. The tendons in his neck were visible as he strained against their grasp, but he couldn't work himself free. They pulled him higher, further, until he was plastered against the ceiling, his arms and legs pulled taut. Louis released a final scream before he was pulled through the metal like it was water.

"Louis!" Cordelia screamed.

Marigold grabbed her wrist and bolted down the hallway, the pain in her leg forgotten for now.

"I know how to get up there."

It took a moment for Rene to shake himself out of his stupor and pursue them. The staircase wobbled under them as they clambered up to the next floor. The song of the cello blared through the halls, mixing with shrieked laughter and the raging gale beyond the wall.

The path they had to take made them weave back and forth to get to the room above Marigold's cabin. They barreled into the room to find Louis on the floor, shaking and panting for breath. A man hovered over him, his feet never touching the ground. Grey and rotting, the specter loomed over Louis as he cringed away. It seemed to take most of Louis's strength just to lift his head and look in their direction.

Marigold's focus was upon Louis. The ghost hovered in her peripheral vision, lean and long, like a serpent ready to strike. Not forgotten, but not as important and the man laid broken on the ground. Time seemed to slow, existing between heartbeats as they each waited to see what the others might do. The ghost lifted its face. The dark recesses that were once its eyes fixed on the three by the door, seeing but unseeing, watching even as it had no eyeballs left to speak of.

Louis grunted as he was suddenly hurled into the air. He careened across the room and slammed into Rene. They both stumbled back across the hallway and collided with the wall. Marigold and Cordelia didn't hesitate. They rushed forward, grabbed the men, and yanked them to the side. Louis was heavy in Marigold's arms, making each step a labor, and her leg threatened to collapse. He tried to work his legs, tried to take some of his weight, but all he could manage was a low scramble across the floor.

She yelled out directions as they ran. Every second of the journey, Marigold was certain that one of them would be taken again. Snatched away and carried to another part of the boat, perhaps never to be seen again. She was sure that the ghost would appear again and rip Louis from her arms. Her fingers clenched his shirt and he wrapped an arm around her waist, his grip firm even as his fingers trembled. They weaved their way through the hallways, their feet thundering against the floor. The wind outside grew louder, transforming into screams of anguish and pain. They lumbered through the large double doors of the ballroom, Rene and Cordelia slammed them shut as Marigold and Louis toppled onto the floor. They barricaded the doors as best they could, shoved broken chairs and mangled tables in the way. Everything they could find was pulled in front of it and piled high. Louis shivered as he tried to get onto his hands and knees. A light sheen of sweat covered his skin, and he could barely lift his head.

"What the hell was that?" Rene said.

Louis swallowed. "Mr. Creeper."

His shirt was damp under Marigold's hand as she rubbed the length of his spine. She couldn't tell whether the wet cloth was because of her own drenched clothes or because of his sweat. He leaned into the touch and slumped back to sit down on the floor.

"Are you okay?" Marigold whispered, not wanting to startle him.

He loosely nodded. "I don't want to do that again."

The wind grew to an ear-splitting howl, the boat trembled, the rows of windows rattled within their frames. Shadows began to streak past the fogged glass. The metal around them groaned as the shadows began to congeal along the edges. They darkened and swelled, shaping themselves into reaching hands that clawed over the wall. The hands of fathomless, glistening black reached through the glass, growing in numbers until they choked off the last traces of light.

CHAPTER 14

Louis couldn't shake the sensation of a thousand spiders burrowing under his skin. They scurried over his trembling limbs, sparked across his nerve endings, and made his skin prickle and twitch. Blood oozed out of the claw marks that streaked across his back. It beaded against his raw skin and soaked into his shirt. He watched as the arms choked off the last rays of light. Darkness rushed to fill the room, smothering all traces of sound and touch with it. He curled his fingers but could no longer feel the floor. Temperature no longer existed, and while he could breathe, he could no longer feel the air fill his lungs. All traces of scent disappeared and he could no longer taste his salty sweat upon his lips. It was complete sensory deprivation. Nothing existed beyond the pain that sizzled along his back and the rapid, panicked breathing of the others.

"Louie," Cordelia trembled out his name as a silent plea for reassurance.

He longed to tell her that it was okay, that it wasn't what she thought, but while the lie would bring comfort, it wouldn't change anything. Even as he tried to keep his voice soft, his words echoed within the now silent room.

"They're almost through the boundaries."

Rene said, "So what do we do?"

Even in the complete darkness, Louis felt them watching him, waiting, expecting him to know exactly what to do. Out of all of them, he had the most experience with ghosts. They needed him to have the answer. Needed him to know how they could survive. He racked his brains, dredging up every memory he could, but he couldn't find the solution they wanted.

The room rattled as something struck the door in a series of thunderous booms. They all scrambled back from the vibrating door, blindly staring in its direction. No one dared to breathe as the pounding stopped and they sank back into devouring silence. Louis flinched when fingers timidly brushed against his own. A heartbeat later, he realized that it was Marigold and reached back for her. The position put more strain on his hip, but he tightened his grip on her trembling hand. Her skin was cool and soft against his as her long fingers gripped him with surprising strength. The contact was a small measure of comfort but one he gladly took. He squeezed her back, unable to see her, but heard her shuffle closer to his side.

The sharp, resonating pounding began again. They jumped with each strike, the impact resounding within his ribcage, and Marigold's grip tightened to the point of pain. He wanted to draw her closer, but his body refused to move. The whispering started softly, a thousand voices layering over each other until the meaning was lost in the noise. Like the senseless buzz of white noise, the whispers grew louder, filling every inch of air.

"What is it saying?" Cordelia whispered.

Rene mumbled something, the words lost in the increasing white noise. They came from everywhere at once, but suddenly a voice spoke directly into his ear, crisp and clear.

Kill her and live.

Each voice repeated the same sentence over and over, sometimes with joyful glee, while others drenched with screeching rage.

Kill her and live.

Marigold's hand tightened until her nails broke his skin, and Louis realized he wasn't the only one who heard it.

Kill her and live.

The voices broke into demanding, wild screams. He pressed his free hand to his ear, but it offered no relief. The voices coiled around his brain like barbwire. They screamed from within his skull, the unrelenting words driving him to the ground.

Kill her!

Light exploded behind Louis's eyelids as the voices roared. He flattened himself against the ground, broken under the onslaught, the marrow of his bones vibrating with the sound. His muscles clenched and he dragged himself into a tight ball. Somewhere, beyond the voices that felt like lava dripping into his ears, he felt Marigold's hands upon him. She was speaking, but her words couldn't compete with the noise that filled him to the brim and left him reeling and strained his muscles to the point of snapping.

Within a second, he was released. He slumped to the floor, desperately gulping in an attempt to fill his lungs. Thin traces of light hit his eyelids, the soft glow like a spike driving through his eyes. Trying to hide from the light, he pressed his throbbing forehead to the moldy carpet, the musty smell of mildew filling his nose. Sound had come back to the world and he was able to hear Marigold calling to him. She was by his side, rocking his shoulder as gently as if he were glass. Still, each jolt made his brain slosh as if it were caught in a breaking swell.

"Louis," she begged, her voice laced with barely restrained tears.

He peeled his eyes open and stared at the carpet as they slowly adjusted to the newly regained light. When the pain subsided, he turned to face her and gave her hand a reassuring squeeze.

"Can you hear me?" She dipped down to fill his view.

Unsure that he was able to speak, Louis nodded carefully, attempting to keep the movement too slow to bring another onslaught of nausea. Still, bile worked its way up his throat, forcing him to swallow repeatedly to fight off the urge to vomit.

"Are you okay?" Marigold asked in a whisper.

The fingers of her free hand were blissfully cool as she flittered over the overheated skin of his neck. Louis let his eyelids fall and took a moment to enjoy the contact. It smothered the lingering traces of pain and silenced the tracing voices that repeated their command. It seemed like she couldn't decide where to touch him, or if she should. She handled him like she thought he would shatter under the slightest amount of pressure.

"Louis?"

His lips quirked at the horrible mispronunciation of his name and he forced his eyes back open. This time, when the slight nod didn't churn his stomach, he took the risk to speak.

"I'm okay, Cher. Are you?"

"Yeah," she forced out on a panted breath.

"Help me up?"

It took both of them to return him to a sitting position. He braced his forearms against his knees and cradled his head. *At least the spiders are gone,* he thought to himself. It was a small mercy, but one he was eternally thankful for. Hands no longer clogged the windows and the tainted light washed into the room, only hindered by the dirt upon the glass and the fog beyond. In the dim glow, Louis spotted Rene and Cordelia a few feet away, they leaned heavily against each other and were constantly reassuring one another that they were okay. He caught Cordelia's eyes and she gently smiled at him. He smiled back as best as he could.

"What happened?" Marigold asked.

Rene snapped his head up and his face instantly paled with the need to vomit. He pushed through the sensation to speak, but kept the words quick and flat, like he was worried to keep his mouth open for too long.

"You didn't hear any of that?"

"Any of what? The knocking?" Marigold asked with clear desperation.

"You didn't hear the voices?" Cordelia said.

Marigold shook her head in bafflement, her eyes skirting between them all. "What voices? What were they saying?"

All eyes fell upon Louis and he bit his lips. "It doesn't matter, Maggie."

"It was telling us that if we kill you, it will let us go," Rene said. The man met Louis's glare with a calmed demeanor and added, "I think she has a right to know."

"You weren't going to tell me that?" Marigold demanded.

Each word thundered in Louis's head, and he rested his forehead back down against his palms. "I was going to tell you when you told me about the corpses."

"Sass isn't a good look on a man," Cordelia chastised.

He waved her off. "There's no reason to tell her since it's a stupid demand that no one is going to fulfil."

"So, we're not even gonna talk it out?" Even when faced with all of their glares, Rene refused to back down, his face a perfect mask. "I'm still playing catch-up here, but even I understand that it's only a matter of time before that demon," his mouth curled around the word like it left a foul taste, "gets in here. What will it do to us when that happens? And I can't be the only one who noticed that the things at the windows are gone. Why would they leave? It's waiting on something, it's waiting to see what we'll do, and if doing what it wants is our only chance of surviving, we need to toss the idea about."

"It's playing a mind game," Louis said with controlled calm. "That's what it does. This particular demon has a fetish for forcing people to inflict pain on others. To break them down until they're willing to kill. At least try and give it a challenge, Rene."

"Does any of that change what the outcome of this situation will be?" Rene said. "If we hold out, will it leave us alone? Or will it kill us too? Because I'm not all too certain you can keep it out."

"We only have to hold out until dawn," Cordelia said. "The ghosts will be weaker then. Without Poppy acting as a guard dog, we'll be able to hike to the nearest town for help."

"So it's just going to let us go?"

Her eyes narrowed. "We're not killing Marigold. How are you even contemplating that?"

Rene didn't look away. "How are you not?"

"You're being scary and disturbing, sugar. Now would be a good time to stop talking."

"If I have to kill Marigold to keep you safe, I'll do it." He turned his attention to Marigold. Louis instinctively tightened his hold on her hand, drawing her closer. "It's nothing personal."

"I understand," Marigold mumbled.

"You're both insane and we're not having this conversation," Louis snapped. He continued before Rene could respond, "It's never a good idea to do what a demon wants you to do. As a general rule, do the opposite. Really, I shouldn't have to explain that."

"Fine," Rene said. "Then what's your plan?"

"What?"

"If even the notion is so far out of the question, I'm guessing that you have an alternative. So, what is it? What do we do now?"

Louis held Rene's demanding gaze for as long as he could. But eventually, he turned to Cordelia and mumbled, "I can't keep it out. I don't have the equipment or the skill."

"So, what do we do?" Rene pressed.

Louis tumbled through his own thoughts, but his mind was still a garbled mess. Every case he had ever experienced, every book he had ever read, every story and urban legend he had ever been told, all bubbled to the surface of his thoughts. There had to be something. Anything. A cold breeze swept up his spine as one option rose above the others. It was a horrible choice and yet he still found himself meeting Cordelia's gaze with conviction.

"We trap it."

He had hoped that she might not have understood the connotations of what he was suggesting, but his cousin's eyes instantly widened and she froze. With a breathy, disbelieving laugh, she shook her head. Rene either didn't notice or care about Cordelia's reaction and was quick to jump on the idea.

"That's an option?" he asked.

"Normally, you would need a graveyard. But the corpses in the water could work," Louis replied. "And it is a location of death. Together that might be enough to make it work. We have a chance to pull it off."

Marigold turned to face him fully. "Why haven't we tried that before?"

"Because it's an insane idea," Cordelia said in a firm voice. "Louie, this is a demon. Why on earth would you think you know how to do this?"

"I've seen it done."

"In person?"

Louis hesitated and hoped that Cordelia didn't notice or question. "In videotapes."

"Great uncle Marius's tapes?" His stomach lurched. Of course, she knew. "Our great uncle who was removed from our family tree with a vengeance? Have you lost your little mind?"

"Who was Marius?" Marigold asked.

"He was a conjurer," Louis said.

"He was a Satanist who dabbled in black magic," Cordelia corrected. "Who even let you touch those tapes?"

"The point is that I've seen them, and it's something you remember. I know how to do it."

"You're talking about blood magic. Dark conjuring. Auntie would slap you silly if she ever heard that you were even *thinking* about this. And if you don't watch yourself, I'm going to take a few swings myself."

Louis held her eyes. "Do you have a better option?"

"Slathering yourself in chicken innards and going for a swim in the bayou is a better option," she shot back. "There has to be another way."

"Trapping it seems like a good thing," Rene said.

"That's because you have no idea what's going on." Cordelia's rage grew, but her tone could never be described as anything but polite. "This is dangerous."

"I severed its connection to Marigold," Louis said. "For it to be this strong, it has to be feeding off something. It's got a strong connection to an energy that's pure, raw, and strong, and unless we get rid of that, we're never going to get rid of it. But if we trap it, that connection will automatically be severed. We'll be able to exorcise it, once and for all."

"So you're saying you want to try and trap a fully formed and well-fed demon?" Cordelia paused for a moment. "Come over here, I want to smack the silly out of you."

"I'm saying that our options are very limited right now. Rene is right, in a way. When it gets in here, it won't be merciful. We need to do something drastic."

Cordelia shook her head, her pretty features twisting in barely suppressed anger even as Rene tried to calm her.

"Trapping it can't be a bad idea," Marigold said.

"At least no one will have to die," Rene added.

Rage flashed in Cordelia's eyes and she turned to Louis. "Go on then," she said. "Tell them what we're going to put it in."

"Do we need a box?" Rene asked. "Or like a kid's toy? They always seem to get possessed in the movies."

"Oh, no," Cordelia said with forced cheerfulness. "This demon is far too strong for that. And besides, Great Uncle never liked doing things that way."

"So what would you put it in?" Marigold asked.

Louis took a deep breath and met her eyes. "Me."

CHAPTER 15

Marigold felt like her insides had been hollowed out in one vicious pull. She stared at Louis as the words repeated in her head. No matter how many times she heard them, she couldn't get them to make sense. They had been fighting and bleeding for months to keep it out of her, and now he was offering *himself* up. He didn't look away, his hazel eyes meeting hers with challenge and determination.

"You're going to let it inside of you?" she asked softly, barely able to force her mouth to make the words.

"I've been possessed before. I know I can take it."

Cordelia's voice cracked like a whip. "Inviting the benevolent Ioa deities to enter you during voodoo rituals is a completely different situation from having this thing carved out of evil crammed inside of you." She whirled on Rene and jabbed a finger against his chest. "And I swear, if you make some kind of smartass comment right now, I'm filing for divorce."

"I can do this," Louis insisted.

"Have you forgotten what demonic possession is?" When she failed to get a reaction out of Louis, Cordelia turned her attention to Marigold. "It eats you. Like a parasite, like a disease. It destroys your memories, your personality, your beliefs. It makes your very sense of self, fester inside of you. It rots you from the inside out. And when you have nothing left, it devours your soul."

"Stop this," Louis said.

Cordelia didn't look away from Marigold's eyes. "Are you going to let him do that?"

"This isn't on her."

"If you're not going to listen to me, reason, common sense, or your self-preservation instinct, maybe you'll listen to her."

"I don't hear you offering another option," Louis said.

"It doesn't want you, Louis. It will fight."

He tried to dismiss the words. "I've annoyed it a bit."

"That just makes it worse," Cordelia snapped.

"You said it yourself," Louis cut in. "We just need to survive until dawn. We do the ritual—"

"The banned blood magic conjuring," Cordelia corrected.

Louis released a slow breath and continued, "Yes. That. We trap it inside me. I hold it until dawn, and then we get Ma to get it out."

"Oh, of course, I've forgotten how easy exorcisms are." Cordelia rolled her eyes.

"The only other option on the table is to kill Marigold. I'm not going to let that happen."

Marigold looked between the relatives. During the argument, Louis had released her hand. She now twisted her fingers around themselves until her knuckles strained, a moment away from dislocating. She swallowed thickly but finally found her breath.

"Why not me?"

Louis whirled around to face her. "What?"

"Why don't we put it in me? It wants me. Reason says it won't fight as much."

"No," Louis said sharply. His tone left no room for argument, but she pushed forward anyway.

"It's better than it going into you."

"How?" Louis said. "It wants to destroy you."

"Doesn't it want to destroy everyone?" Rene asked.

Louis gnashed his teeth as he glared at the man. "Stay out of this."

"It makes more sense for it to be me," Marigold persisted. "I won't know what to do to it when it has you, and I'm not strong enough to restrain you."

"Maggie, the process is dangerous. You could die."

"Funny how you didn't mention that when we were discussing

putting it inside you." Cordelia received the same reaction for her intrusion as Rene had.

Marigold reached out and grabbed his wrist, forcing his attention back to her.

"It's going to be okay."

"No," Louis said. "And you can't make me do it."

"No, but I can choose to back Rene's plan."

Louis raked a hand over his head. "I know things look helpless, but you can't just jump to suicide."

"I don't want to die," Marigold said as she squeezed his wrist. "But I'm not going to let you die for me. I brought all of this upon you."

"It's not your fault."

"But I did it," she said. Louis lowered his head and squeezed his eyes. "I can do this. Just let me help you, Louis."

He tried to smile but couldn't make it happen. "You're still pronouncing that wrong."

The silence that lingered within the room was destroyed by the return of the screaming wind. The windows rattled and the room trembled. The scattered tables rattled across the ballroom floor, the rested metal scraping against the wood. They all scrambled for purchase as the boat heaved. Louis didn't wait for the quake to pass before he lifted his gaze to meet Marigold. He knew she saw the defeat that was turning his bones to stone, but he still tried to hide his fear, his disgust. It wasn't just the risk that drove him to the brink of being violently ill. The spell demanded things he wasn't quite sure he could bring himself to do. But they were desperate. He hated himself for letting it come to this. The floor settled and Marigold tightened her fingers around his wrist.

She took a deep breath. "What do we need to do?"

Marigold took pride in the amount of strength she had managed to put into the question. She didn't feel an ounce of it. But she couldn't let him see. If he knew how terrified she was, he would insist on taking her place.

"I'll need a knife," Louis mumbled as he skirted his eyes to Rene. "Do you still have the meat cleaver?"

Rene held it up. His attempt to make the motion look casual failed because of his obvious white knuckled grip.

"What else?" Cordelia refused to look at anyone as she said the words, her shoulders hunched and her face low.

"A candle, blood, some free space, and something flammable that I can draw on," he licked his lips and forced himself to continue. "We'll also need a way to restrain her once it's done."

Cordelia glanced over his shoulder to the ballroom. "We have a lot of tablecloths?"

"I think I've still got some candles in the bar at the back," Marigold said as she got to her feet.

Her socks squished against the floor with her every step. Cordelia retrieved a tablecloth as Rene pushed aside a bunch of tables and chairs to clear a space in the middle of the room. Brushing the layer of dead leaves aside, Louis used the meat cleaver to scratch into the floorboards. His brow furrowed as he concentrated, making each symbol from memory. Marigold tried not to think about it. About what it meant.

It's going to be bad. It's going to hurt, a voice in her head whispered despite her attempts to ignore it. Louis wouldn't study satanic practices. He wouldn't remember it by choice. Whatever he had seen on that tape had burnt itself into his memory like a branding iron.

Dropping onto her knees, Marigold sorted through the boxes that were packed under the flimsy counter. She couldn't quite remember where she had put the candles, but she knew they were there. She pushed aside a few lanterns and crumbling cardboard boxes, finally finding the small box of candles and matchbox tucked away in a corner. She ran back just as Rene and Cordelia settled the blanket into place.

Marigold could feel Louis's eyes on her, watching her carefully as she scattered the candles. His mouth was pressed into a fine line as he nervously picked at the cleaver's chipped handle. When the candles were lit and everything else was in position, Marigold turned to him for the next task. He lowered his eyes.

"Blood, right," Marigold said as a sinking pit opened up in her stomach. "You need mine."

"Just a little," he mumbled.

His jaw twitched and he lowered his face further. Her gentle smile of reassurance was lost as he refused to look at her face. She knelt down and presented her hand.

"It'll be alright in the end," she said.

His lips jerked as he closed his eyes. "We just have to keep going until we get there, yeah?"

"Exactly."

Louis delicately cupped the back of her hand, his skin warm and solid. A gentle caress. The blade of the knife bit at the skin of her palm. Louis moved as quickly as he could, his fingers massaging the back of her hand like he could ease the pain. He instructed her on how to spread the blood, the symbols she needed to create across the tablecloth. She didn't recognize any of them and dirt began to gather in the wound.

"Shit," he mumbled when they were almost finished.

Her stomach lurched at his sudden cuss and she spun around to face him. Louis was looking to Cordelia.

"We forgot the animal."

Rene looked between them. "You need an animal? Like as a sacrifice?"

"Its cries of pain wake up the spirits," Cordelia said. "It makes them pay attention."

The rugged man didn't attempt to keep the disgust from his face. "You torture animals?"

"Not for fun," Cordelia snapped. "It's a necessary part of the ceremony. And in normal rituals, we'll honor the sacrificed animal by cooking it and sharing it as a meal."

"I'm not sure I want to eat it."

"You won't have to," Louis said. "For this ceremony, I just need to inflict pain on something, the bigger the better."

"So, we need an animal," Rene shifted his attention to the windows. "Isn't it just funny how we're surrounded by swamps infested with critters but we can't get any of them? We might be able to find a snake lurking around."

"I'd prefer a gator," Louis said.

Marigold fought the urge to clasp her wounded hand against her chest. She didn't want to look weak as she said, "What about me?"

Rene's eyes narrowed on her. "Do you have a volunteering obsession or something?"

"Marigold," Cordelia said gently, "you can't."

"Well, not the killing part. But it's the pain you need, right? Without it, this whole thing is just a twisted waste of time, right?"

Louis had become rigid and spoke in a dull tone she had never heard. "You can't ask me to do that."

Marigold bit her lips, her mind telling her to speak while her body cringed away from carrying on.

"When the demon's inside of me," she started slowly, "it will be able to use me to hurt people, right? Or run away so you can't force it back out?"

Rene turned around. "I'm going to check again for rope."

Marigold continued, "It would make sense to incapacitate me."

"What are you thinking?" Cordelia asked in place of Louis.

He looked drained of color and he didn't seem to blink.

"Break my legs."

"What?" he snapped. "I can't do that."

"Don't you do that for the rituals?" she challenged.

"I'm not a priest. I don't run the ceremonies. I never actually had to do any of it."

"Well, now you do," Cordelia said. "The possession was your suggestion. This is what it takes."

"I can't," he said softly.

"There's no point in doing this if it doesn't end up protecting anyone," Marigold said. "I don't want to hurt you. And I don't want this thing stuck in me."

"We have to make sure it doesn't escape," Cordelia agreed.

"Then you do it," he snapped.

"You're doing the spell, it has to be you."

He turned to Marigold, his eyes begging, but she could only give him a reassuring smile. Squeezing his eyes shut he nodded sharply.

"We'll find something big. Heavy. We'll do it quickly."

"Okay." She managed to keep her smile even as her insides twisted and squirmed.

She wanted to take it back as Louis instructed her to lay down on the sheet. Her heart hammered and her palms began to sweat. The salt mingled with her cut, making it sting with a renewed ache. *I guess I'll need that tetanus shot,* her mind babbled abruptly. She clenched her hands and let the smile tug on her lips. Picking a place on the ceiling, she fixed her eyes on it and refused to look anywhere else. Shadows shifted as the ground shook again. They had to hold onto the candles to keep them upright. Hot wax splashed across her arms, but she didn't move away. When the rattling stopped, she could hear something heavy being dragged towards her. *To break your legs,* her mind supplied. *Or to lock you in after.* She squeezed her eyes shut and fought past the lump forming in her throat. She didn't want to see it.

Whatever it was, they dropped it close by her side. Vibrations rattled the floor and sunk into her skin. Her breath caught and she balled her hands despite the pain. *There's going to be a lot more than that.* Panic surged in her chest, growing and burning. Eyes still closed she focused on her breathing, not allowing herself to think about what was about to happen, what the best outcome would be. Air slipped past the scars that lined her throat and expanded her lungs. She listened to the metal groan as it tried to withstand the growing wind that bombarded the ship. Blood, hot and slick, seeped around through her fingers and dripped onto the sheet below her. All the peace she had managed to garnish disappeared when she heard Louis speak.

"We have to start now."

CHAPTER 16

In theory, the plan sounded simple enough, at least to her. All Marigold really had to do was lay there. *Lay there and endure,* she told herself. *Be still. Don't make it harder for him.* She didn't know what would happen if Louis was unable to finish. She didn't ask any questions beyond what they needed her to do. Details would only make it worse. Once it was inside of her, Cordelia would wrap her in the sheet she was laying on, Rene tied her up with everything he had found, and they would all hope that it would be enough to hold her until they could get help. Louis reasoned that there would be an opening, a period of time that it would take for the demon to adjust to her body. If they could get back to a cell service area, they would be able to call Louis's mother before it gained control.

The best-case scenario was that, since no one had checked in, the voodoo priestess would already be on her way. It was an option that Louis desperately clung to. He kept telling her that once Ma was here, everything will be fine. That all they had to do was make the call and they would be able to start the exorcism within a few hours. He repeated the words over and over, as if saying them enough would make them true. Marigold doubted that a single person present believed him, but it was a nice lie, so no one argued with him.

Marigold took a deep breath, her eyes closed, and her fingers shifted. "What do you think it's going to be like? To have it in my flesh with me?"

"I've heard it's different for everyone," Louis said. "There's no way to tell."

"Do you think I'll remember it when your mother gets it out of me?" she asked. "Or do you think it will be like waking up from a dream?"

"I'm hoping it's going to be like coming out of surgery. You'll hurt, but it won't seem like any time has passed at all."

She smiled and took a steadying breath. "I like that." Tears were burning her eyes as her breath shivered. "Promise you'll be here when I wake up?"

"I promise."

Stay still, she commanded herself as Louis began to speak in a language she hadn't heard before. His voice dipped and rose like he was conducting a performance upon a stage. Lead filled her chest. *Stay still.* Metal scraped against metal as they moved the item into place. She ached to look. No good would come from seeing what was about to break her. *You can do this. Stay still. Don't look.*

Louis's voice became a bellow that raged over the hurricane wind outside. Metal scraped. She heard her bone crack an instant before her brain registered the pain. There wasn't enough air in her lungs to scream as her back arched off the floor. Her hands clutched at her right leg, protectively wrapping herself around it as tears burned her eyes. Cordelia grabbed her shoulders and pushed her back down.

"We still have to do the other leg," she whispered to Marigold.

Marigold ground her teeth against her pleas for them to stop. Agony pulsed through her leg, rushing to fill every inch of her being. She whined and clutched Cordelia's arm as she forced herself to straighten.

"We'll be quick," she heard Cordelia promise in a whisper.

The windows shattered under the pressure of the wind. Glass shards rained down, sounding like hail as they hit the floor. The wind rushed in through the empty space. She felt it whip her as the ghastly wail rang in her ears. *You can't stop now,* she told herself firmly before she gave a single nod. She could barely hear Louis shout over the gale.

"Make sure you scream," Cordelia whispered as the sound of scraping metal came once more.

It slammed down, shattering her left leg. Her body jerked as she screamed. Every slight shift of the rocking boat sent a new spasm of pain slicing through her body. She didn't try to hold back her cries and sobs. The pressure was removed, replaced by hands that grabbed her legs and squeezed. Spit dribbled from her mouth as she cried. Her nails shredded the sheets as she writhed and trembled.

The wind howled, drowning out Louis's words. *Louis.* She forced her eyes open but couldn't see past her tears. Louis was moving, walking around her slowly as he continued to perform the ceremony. While she didn't understand the words, she felt the power of them. The floor steadily grew hotter until it scorched her back. By the time Louis reached her head, her screams had broken into shattered sobs.

The hands squeezed again, forcing another scream from her raw throat. Her eyes bulged, and her neck strained, and it took everything she had to keep still. The sheets twisted around her hands as she struggled. The doors quaked as something solid slammed into them. The knocking grew louder, harder, mixing with the wail of the wind and Louis's continued commands.

Louis knelt down next to her. His hand pressed against Marigold's forehead. Blinking past the agony that consumed her, the unshed tears blurred her vision, she caught sight of her. His fingers trembled against her skin. He met her eyes and his voice began to crack. It terrified her to close her eyes, to lose the limited connection, but she forced herself to do so. He needed her to.

"It's okay," Marigold whispered to him. "I'm okay. Keep going."

She heard him suck in a rattling breath and his words became stronger. *Stay still,* she told herself. *He won't get through this if you don't.* She swallowed thickly and kept her eyes sealed tight. The hands on her shins had never left, but they had stilled. Now they began to squeeze and twist her legs, grinding the fractured bones against each other. Marigold's body tried to lurch up, physically forcing her screams out of her, but Louis's hand kept her head against the floor, holding her in place.

The doors rattled violently. The scent of the blown-out candles swirled around her. The cold wind snapped the sheet sharply against her as the floor continued to heat. Sweat began to pool along her back. Through the tears in the sheet, she could feel the floorboards splinter and crack like an inferno lay below her. It began to burn her skin. She flinched her hands away from the gaps, but the sheet offered her little protection.

Louis's hand shifted. His fingers balled in her hair and yanked her head back, exposing the long column of her throat. She felt the sharp edge of the meat cleaver press against the swelled scar across her throat. A new terror rushed through her. *Stay still. Stay still.* It felt like the scar was splitting open with the strain. Her fingers clawed at the sheet, but she managed to keep her shoulders and head in place. With each breath, she was sure the blade would sink into her skin. The blade lifted and she tumbled into a fit of sobs.

The cool slip of metal pressed against her sternum. She held her breath but it pushed harder against her anyway. The thin layer of her shirt offered little protection. Once again it lifted. Louis's palm against her forehead faded away, only to be replaced by the blade. Blood swelled around the meat cleaver that sliced into her skin. It pooled and trailed down into her hair. She could almost hear each drop sizzle as it hit the sweltering floor. Her nose was filled with the stench of smoke and raw meat. *Stay still. Stay still.*

Cordelia screamed as Marigold felt the first flickers of flame licking at her wrist. She pulled away before she could stop herself, the jolt forcing the blade deeper into her skin. Blood gushed forward from the new wound as Cordelia fought to pat out the small flames that now littered the sheet.

Stay still.

The doors burst open with a thunderous crack that shook the room.

Stay still.

Hands, as cold as ice and each finger tipped with a talon, grabbed her ankles and yanked. Marigold pushed her head up, not feeling the pain as the knife ripped her skin again. A black mass hovered over her feet. It was as formless as smog but thick enough that she couldn't see through it. She couldn't breathe; her head and lungs screamed in protest. The shadow lifted its head. Gaping holes stood in the place of eyes, but she could feel its gaze upon her. A smile split its head in two, exposing rows of rotten fangs.

Marigold screamed and tried to wrench herself free. But the creature held tight. Her jerked movements twisted her broken legs, grinding the bones together, and she released a scream that shattered her at her core. Hands climbed up her body, the claws sinking deep into her flesh. The floor boiled against her back. The weight of the shadow pressed her down.

Mine. The single word hit her ears even as it rolled in her mind. She thrashed and strained, but she couldn't dislodge the weight, the claws. Sobs wracked her. She wanted to run. *You can't do this. You're not strong enough.* The words were within her skull, but she could no longer tell if the thought was her own.

Mine. Its rancid breath ghosted over her neck. Its weight against her knees created constant waves of agony. She tried to stay still. It only hurt more when she moved. But she couldn't stop herself from screaming, from crying.

"Stay still," she couldn't hear her voice over the howl of the wind.

Forcing her eyes open she looked back, desperately searching for Louis. He knelt behind her head, still chanting, the blade of his knife dipped in her blood. He wouldn't look at her, but instead stared at a spot on the floor with unwavering intensity. Each word cost him, made him shake and sweat. Tears clung to his lashes.

Look at me, she begged him silently. *See me.* She needed to know he was there with her. Needed to know that she wasn't alone. But he kept his eyes fixed away from her. It was impossible to hear anything over the wind, but he still flinched at her every scream. *Look at me. Stay with me.* It felt like her throat was bleeding, and she choked on it. The skin of her back boiled while the touch of the demon felt like the burn of dry ice. The demon's voice slithered in her head, a whisper heard over the chaos that existed beyond her skin.

I see you. She squeezed her eyes shut but could not do anything to drown out the noise. Unseen claws pressed against her lips. They shredded her tender skin as they forced themselves into her mouth. Blood spewed across her tongue as the clawed fingers forced her mouth open. Her jaw ached and her skin stretched to the point of splitting. Putrid sludge poured into her, filling every inch before it began to slide down her throat.

The scar of her neck burned as her spine cracked and bowed, leaving her tittering on the tips of her toes and the crown of her head. The sheets bunched under her hands as she tried to find something to hold onto, something to steady herself with. The shadow clawed down her throat, past her lungs and deeper into her stomach. She could feel it hollowing her out to make room. The pain was beyond anything that her legs had created. Marigold gagged, helplessly trying to wrench the creature from her, but it was no use. It only burrowed deeper. Her lungs burned as she shook with the pain. She could only sob and choke.

Cordelia was by her side, her hands trying to force her back down. Marigold heard someone screaming but couldn't understand the words. Rene hovered at the edge of her vision, his face twisted with shock as he watched Marigold struggle, but she couldn't see Louis. Then the blanket moved. One side at a time was thrown over her head. The material bunched and bulked as it covered the demon slithering down her throat. More chaos and screams. Heavy strips of cord fell across her. They were trying to pull her down, but it was no use. Her toes brushed against the floorboards before she rose into the air. Her hair fell in mattered tendrils, swaying in the last gasps of the breeze as she floated a few feet off the ground.

The last of the shadow scrambled inside and released her airway. Her lungs sucked in a deep breath, her spine bowing more under the force until she was almost folded in two. Her eyes widened, but she couldn't see anything beyond the stained and tattered sheet that hung over her, the ends snapping in the swirling breeze. The strips around her tightened and tugged but did nothing.

Mine.

Light burst behind her eyes, her body snapped, and gravity once again claimed her. With a broken gasp, she began to fall.

CHAPTER 17

Louis's knees gave out and he collapsed to the floor, sweat cooling against his skin. He couldn't look away from the bundle of sheets that covered the now limp form of Marigold. The only movement was the soft rise and fall that signified that she was breathing. Her blood began to seep into the sheet, looking black in the orange-tinged light. The stench of burnt flesh and smoke filled the room, and the quiet night was slowly claimed by the chatter of frogs and insects. Louis watched as Rene and Cordelia hurriedly tied up Marigold with the odd pieces of cord and wire that they had been able to find. The sheet pulled tighter around her slight form. It looked like they were wrapping up a corpse. Rene began to tighten the sheet into place around her neck and Louis scrambled forward.

"Don't. She won't be able to breathe."

"She also won't be able to bite us," Rene said dismissively.

Louis grabbed Rene's wrist and yanked him back. "I said don't!"

Louis's grip was as strong as iron even as his arms trembled. He didn't look away from Rene's defiant glare.

"Louis," Cordelia snapped. "We need to go."

"He's going to kill her," Louis said.

Rene yanked his arm out of Louis's grip and growled.

"Hand me the cleaver and I'll cut her a breathing hole. Good compromise?"

Louis didn't say anything but allowed Rene to pull the meat cleaver from his loose grip. The sound of cracking bones repeated in his head. His stomach heaved each time he remembered that thick, wet, crack. Deep breathing didn't help, and he flopped forward, bracing his forearms against the floor as he wretched and choked. He was barely able to keep the contents of his stomach from rushing out of his throat.

"Louis," Cordelia said again as she wrapped an old wire cord around Marigold's legs. *The legs you broke*, his mind reminded him. "We need to go."

Louis nodded as he staggered onto his feet. The phone would still be in Marigold's cabin. If he was quick, perhaps they could get Ma out here before Marigold woke up. Or before it woke up within her skin. His stomach churned again and he braced one hand against the table to steady himself.

"I should have been able to help her. I should have seen it coming."

"Louie, this isn't your fault," Cordelia said.

"Deal with the guilt later," Rene snapped. "Run."

He nodded and surged towards the door. "If she wakes up—"

"We won't listen to a word," Cordelia said. "We won't say a word."

Rene set the last knot in place with a vicious yank and Louis swallowed down the urge to yell at him again. With Louis at Marigold's shoulders and Rene at her feet, they lifted the unconscious body a few feet off the ground. They stubbornly stumbled for a few steps before acknowledging that it wasn't going to work.

"I'll take her," Louis said.

Between the two of them, Rene spent more time doing physical activity, but he didn't complain when Louis took Marigold's weight. His feet felt like stone as he staggered to the side, unbalanced by the sudden weight of Marigold slumped over one shoulder. Rene stayed close long enough to make sure he wasn't going to have to catch them before he turned his attention to Cordelia. Already on her feet and refusing to let go of the meat cleaver, Cordelia pulled Rene into a tight hug. The two separated after a few whispered words and hurried to the barricaded door.

They were still pushing debris aside as Louis caught up. The large doors loomed in the deathly silence. For a moment, they all hesitated, staring at the door handle while not daring to touch it and see what lay on the other side. Eventually, Cordelia wrapped her hand around one door handle, Rene around the other, and they all exchanged a final glance.

"We stick together," Rene's voice was only a whisper, but they didn't struggle to hear him.

In unison, Cordelia and Rene wrenched open the doors, but none of them could force themselves to move. The dimly lit hallway stretched out before them. Calm, silent, and covered with colorful lights that couldn't fight off the shadows.

"Phone first," Rene mumbled. "We grab that rope on the deck on the way out."

They both looked to Cordelia. She adjusted her grip on the meat cleaver's handle, sucked down a deep breath, and then nodded. Taking it as their cue, the men bolted into the hallway, Rene in the front while Cordelia protected them from behind. Their footsteps rattled off the walls and rolled out before them. The ghosts were gone, as if in hiding, but Louis still expected for one of them to slither out from the dark crevasses that littered the hall. They leaped down the last few stairs and raced to the cabin.

Rene was the first one through the door. Louis's stomach cramped at the thought of going back in there, but he forced his feet to move. Marigold's bed was cracked and hung at a limp angle, and the mattress slumped against the opposite wall. As gently as his uncoordinated movements would allow, Louis dropped her onto the mattress and joined Rene in ransacking the room. They hurriedly threw aside the broken items and tattered remains of all that Marigold owned as Cordelia lingered in the threshold as a look out. Rene found the phone under a chunk of the destroyed skin. The screen was cracked and the battery was running low, but it seemed to be working. Louis held it tightly, the small device solid against his palm as he reached for Marigold again. It was easier to get her into the fireman carry this time, and they sprinted the remaining distance to the back deck. A huge hole had been ripped into the wall opposite the doorway into the kitchen. The room itself sat in tense silence, and they jumped over the odd items that littered the floor.

A burning ache had seeped into Louis's shoulder by the time they reached the back door. The wood hung off of its hinges, creating a wide enough gap for them to get out. Rene leaped through the space and out into the night air. The fog stirred at his presence, swirling around him as he reached back in to take Marigold. As careful as they were, they couldn't keep the unconscious girl from hitting against the walls. Free from the extra weight, Louis was able to slip around the door, Cordelia close behind. The fog felt like ice as it brushed against their fevered skin, a calming relief that helped to sober that promised freedom and safety, but gave neither. Rene had already found the thick rope and was in the process of weaving it around Marigold's body when Cordelia and Louis found him. The rope pulled tight against the sheets. It looked like they were preparing to bury Marigold at sea. It didn't take long for Rene's skilled fingers to make the final knot. Louis edged closer to take Marigold again, but Rene waved him off.

"I got her."

"Are you sure?" Louis asked.

It was hard to read his face in the fog and that just made Louis's stomach tighten all the more.

"You might need your hands free," Rene finally said as he stood.

He threw Marigold over his broad shoulder with ease and they hurried to join Cordelia at the top of the gangplank.

"Here." Cordelia thrust a flashlight into Louis's hand. She must have gotten it somewhere along the journey, although Louis couldn't remember from where. "The tide would have come in by now."

"I know," Louis said softly. His eyes fixed on the point where the fog swallowed the end of the gangplank.

Rene came up beside him. "The gators will be in. Keep that light off until we get past them."

Louis nodded and cast a final glance at Cordelia.

They looked at each other for a long moment, neither quite sure where to go from here, each still waiting to be blindsided by the mist.

Then Rene smacked Louis on the shoulder and gave him a little shove.

"You keep that phone dry," Rene said as Louis took his first step up onto the rusted gangplank.

It only took a few steps for the fog to sever him from the boat, reducing it to only orbs of light that charged the air. A thick layer of water claimed over half of the metal slip. Hidden under the mist, Louis was only able to see it when he was a few inches from the placid surface. The metal pathway rattled with every step, creating ripples that expanded out and sloshed against things unseen. Louis held the phone safely over his head as the water crept over his body. By the time his feet sank into the mud, the water was already waist high. Progress was slow, not just because he had to struggle for every step, but because he was never quite sure what his foot was going to fall onto, what was lurking under the surface.

The floodlights lit the fog but offered no definition to the world around him. The water reflected the off-color mist until it seemed like that was all that existed. He waited to feel the hard flesh of an alligator, the slip of a snake, or the shifting skin of Poppy's hand. A strong lap of water hit his chest and he froze. Even though he was prepared for it, he still yelped with surprise when something slithered past his leg. His hands tightened on the phone as a shadow emerged from the mist.

Twin eyes shone in the minimal light, little disks of red that grew brighter as the alligator drifted towards them. Cordelia and Rene fell silent. The only sound was the water hitting the side of the boat behind them. Louis closed his eyes and tried to calm his heartbeat. It wouldn't matter in the end. The alligator knew they were there. Even his thoughts spoke in a whisper when it told him, *Marigold is bleeding.* Snapping his eyes open, he glanced to Rene. Apparently, he had come to the same conclusion and now had his hands balled into fists against Marigold's sheet.

The alligator was now close enough for them to see each peak that covered its back like armor. Every muscle in Louis's stomach tightened, and he choked on his breath as the animal drifted within a few feet. The water pressed against him. The world held in silence. And then he felt it, a drag of solid stink and muscle as the side of the alligator slid across him. Louis managed to keep down his yelp but failed to keep himself from flinching at the contact. Eyes still closed, he waited for teeth to rip his skin with bone-crushing strength. Its tail thumped against his hip and he managed to pry his eyes open. He watched as the reptile drifted off, his knees almost buckling.

They waited as long as they could for their journey through the sludge to be continued. The bank was all loosely packed silt, and it swallowed his feet to his ankles. Still, they moved with renewed speed, limping and heaving out of the swamp. Water sloshed from their clothes and drizzled into the mud under them, making it harder to walk. Instantly, the air worked to chill his clothes, and Louis shivered as he hurried forward. The lights of the boat had faded with the distance, giving way to the oppressive night. He fumbled with the flashlight until the small beam flickered to life, but it was of little help. The beam couldn't penetrate the fog and instead just made it brighter.

Unable to get his bearings, Louis blindly but carefully kept moving. Only the road had any real solid structure to it, and he used that as a guide to judge when he moved too far from it. The further he ventured, the thinner the mist became and he was able to make out the shadows of looming trees and swaying Spanish moss. Puddles severed the road. It was hard to spot them in time to keep from barreling into them. The solid gravel gave way to loose soil. It caught up in his feet and made him struggle to keep upright, the beam of the flashlight scattering over the horizon. It was easy to lose track of how far he had run, how long it had been.

They stopped when their lungs began to burn and their legs refused to take another step. Rene struggled to keep from dropping Marigold as he hunched forward and fought to catch his breath. Cordelia took the flashlight from him, scanning it over the shadows around them as Louis turned the phone on, squinting into the bright light that poured from the screen. He had only one bar, barely a signal, but maybe it would be enough. Each button clicked as he dialed, an annoying feature that he hadn't yet figured out how to turn off. His fingers hesitated as the soft sounds of an infant crying hovered in the wind.

Rene and Cordelia both focused on Louis as he turned in desperate circles, trying to locate where the noise was coming from. Cordelia lifted the flashlight and once again scanned the shadows. The mist rolled uninterrupted around the towering trees that surrounded them on all sides.

"Someone tell me they hear that, too," Rene whispered.

"We need to go," Louis said as he broke into a run. He waved his arm to snap the couple out of their bewilderment. "Come on!"

They sprinted after him as his thumb hit the last few digits and connected the call. The gravel crunched under their shoes and their clothes clung to their skin. Louis pressed the phone to his ear until it hurt. His heart sank when the phone offered a few quick beeps. The call hadn't gone through. His lungs began to burn and his muscles clenched. No matter how far or fast he ran, he still felt as if there were something with him, only a few steps behind, the infant's cry screaming in his ears.

The mist thinned and he was able to see traces of moonlight. Trees reached for them with long brittle fingers. Without breaking his stride, Louis hung up and then hit redial. The line buzzed before it beeped again, and he bit back a curse. A sudden cry made both Cordelia and Louis screech to a halt. Cordelia waved the beam to the side, screaming with a frantic edge. "Rene!" She dropped down against the far side of the road, the beam of light fixed on the rippling grass that covered the sinkhole. "Rene!"

Louis bolted forward, dropping the phone as he flattened himself against the gravel road. Pushing his longer torso out onto the unstable surface, he clawed at the plants that sat atop the patch of water that Cordelia eliminated with the flashlight. He ripped out hunks of the tangled green mass, but there always seemed to be more to fill the hole again. The grass bucked as Rene pushed at the underside. Louis drove his fist through the tangled marsh, the roots and vines twisting around his wrist like a thousand snakes. Fingers latched onto his and Louis shot out his free hand to grab Cordelia's arm. She instantly dropped the flashlight and began to yank with every ounce of strength that she could summon.

The plants held firm. Cordelia's heels dug deep into the mud and Louis's joints pulled until they promised to snap. Rene released a rattled gasp as his head broke free of the surface. They dragged him to the edge, unable to get even his shoulders out of the mush. The Cajun heaved each breath, sputtering out mouthfuls of water. He lurched forward as he regained his footing.

"Marigold?" Louis asked.

"Got her." He coughed up another mouthful of water as the algae next to him lifted.

Cordelia pushed forward to hold onto Rene, leaving Louis free to tear through the tangled cluster of weeds again. His skin was shredded by the time he finally found the cloth under the surface. Rene pulled himself out of the water and twisted to help Louis drag Marigold's motionless form out of the water. Louis ripped at the hole in the sheet, forcing it wider to expose Marigold's face.

"Is she breathing?" Cordelia asked.

Louis bent closer and pressed his ear to her chest. He wasn't able to hear her heartbeat over the screams of the phantom infant. With trembling fingers, he pressed against her sternum. The world seemed to stop, hovering within that singular moment until he felt the slight motion of her chest. A slow rise and fall. She was breathing. Louis sagged forward with relief, draping over her and pressing his forehead against her arm.

Rene roughly grabbed the back of Louis's shirt and yanked him away from Marigold. In the same moment, Cordelia grabbed the flashlight, offering her husband the steady glow as he pulled Marigold back onto his shoulder. Snatching up the phone, Louis followed as they once again ran down the only road out of the bayou, their pace slower and every step hurting.

He didn't know how far they had gone when he brought the phone up to his ear and hit the redial button. The trees around them shook, the brittle branches shuttering as something pushed its way through them. Cordelia twisted the beam over the shadows and mist, illuminating the dubby as it shifted in and out of sight while running alongside them. Louis's heart felt like a lump of stone in his chest until he heard the ringing give way to his mother's voice.

"Ma, we need help. I think we just made a huge mistake!"

Before she could ask, he rushed on to explain everything that had happened, the words running into each other in his haste. His legs wobbled, his lungs burned, and exhaustion made it impossible to keep up his pace any longer. Eventually, his body couldn't do what his mind willed it, and he staggered to a stop. Cordelia was the first to notice and slowed her steps to match his, Rene quickly following suit. Unable to catch their breaths, they kept searching the bayou around them for a sign of the ghost that was hunting them.

"I thought you said they couldn't stick around if the demon was trapped," Rene snapped, barely heard over the child's wails.

"He shouldn't be here," Louis said, tightening his grip on the phone until his hand throbbed. This far from the water it was possible to make out a good few feet in any directions. Behind him, the road was relatively clear, and before him, a large puddle expanded the graveled width. To pass it, they would either have to cling to the shadow-drenched trees, or slog through the water and soft ground beneath. The crying abruptly stopped, allowing them to hear the crash of unseen things bursting through the bayou around them. The thin beam of light couldn't illuminate them, only making the fading mist glow.

"Ma, you need to get here now!"

"Louis, honey, put me on speaker phone so everyone can hear me."

Each word was articulated with care, the strange sound slicing through Louis's panic with the threat of something new. He quickly switched the phone onto speaker and drew closer to the others to ensure that they could hear.

"Ma, you have to hurry. I don't know what's going to happen," Louis forced through the lump in his throat. "She's really hurt."

"Calm down, and listen," Ma's overly crisp tone crackled out of the speakers. "The police and I are almost there."

All three of them froze, their blood turning to ice within their veins. Rene crouched next to Marigold's body, unable to catch his breath as blood seeped through the sheet. Even while concealed, it was clear to see that Marigold's legs were twisted at angles they shouldn't be. In the dim light her face was pale, streaked with blood and filth.

Cordelia was the first one to find her voice, "The police? No, they can't see Marigold like this. How are we supposed to explain any of this? You have to keep them away."

"That's right, honey, I have a police officer with me right now," Ma said with exaggerated calmness. "When no one had checked back in with me, I thought that something might have gone wrong. The police officer is giving me a lift out right now." Her voice took on a sweetness that only someone who knew her would know was forced. They each looked at each other as they heard her say to someone else, "Officer, could you radio for an ambulance? My son has just told me that the poor La Roux girl fell and is hurt."

The officer's voice was too mumbled to understand the words, but the volume of it made it clear that the man was pretty close to her. Probably in a driver's seat.

"You guys just stay where you are," Ma went on to give the warning. "We'll be with you in a few minutes."

"Probably earlier," Rene said as he stared at a distant point.

Louis turned to follow his gaze. His lungs turned to iron when he saw the flashing blue and red lights making their way towards them. The fog had concealed the car until they were almost on top of them. There was no time to unravel Marigold. No time to make this look any better than it was.

"Calm down, sweetie, everything will be okay," Ma said. She then spoke to the officer, loud enough to ensure that they could all still hear her as they huddled around the phone.

"Louis says that she was in another room when she got hurt, so they're not sure how long she's been unconscious. There was no reception, so they had to wrap her up to move her. They're worried that it only made the problem worse."

Louis glanced at the others. "She fell," he parroted back the words again, but they tasted like bile in his throat.

"Is anyone going to believe that?" Rene asked.

"We have to make sure that they do," Louis said in a hushed voice. "Or they'll never let us near her. We have to get the demon out of her."

Cordelia jerked back just as a figure emerged from the fog. The dubby drifted closer, its feet hovering over the mush. It only had eyes for Marigold as it lurched closer, teeth bared and eyes glowing. Rene pulled Cordelia behind him as the fog flashed in bursts of red and blue. The police car's breaks squealed. The gravel crunched under the tires and the dubby rushed forward unconcerned. Louis pushed himself between it and Marigold, his skin turning to ice as the dubby loomed over him.

Still unseen, the car doors slammed. The air became thick with energy, sparking and sizzling in the shifting light, creating a static charge that washed out like a shock wave. The dubby halted an inch from Louis's face and looked back over its shoulder. The electric sensation increased until the fog seemed to hum with it.

Ma emerged from the shadows. Louis had always heard of the power that the voodoo priestesses wielded, but he had never actually felt it. She now unleashed the hurricane that she had kept within her skin, and they all cowered back from it. The dubby widened its jaws as the energy surrounding Ma grew into a ferocious wind. The gale stole the dubby's scream as it tore open its flesh. Louis shielded his face as his mother focused her attention on the ghost. It roared and lunged towards Ma. Her power swirled around the ghost before it could get near. It only took a few seconds for the dubby to be ripped apart and scattered in an eruption of sparks.

The police officer turned on the floodlight mounted on the side of the car, the brilliant white glare competed against the rotating lights for dominance. But there was nothing left of the dubby for him to see as he neared. Only a few embers that drifted like golden snow around Ma. Louis could only stare, his chest heaving as his lungs remembered how to function. He was vaguely aware of the police officer's presence. Of the questioning glances and suspicions that he couldn't bring himself to actually voice. Still, his large hand lingered over the hilt of his firearm as Ma rushed forward and dropped down next to Louis. The hand she pressed against his cheek felt the same as it ever had, but now he was painfully aware of the strength that lingered within her skin. It comforted and terrified him at the same time.

"What the hell was that noise?" the officer asked. He rested one hand against the hilt of his holstered weapon as he scanned the scene.

Louis's eyes never left his mother as he fumbled for an excuse. "Skunk ape."

"Skunk ape?" the officer challenged. "The Louisiana bigfoot?"

"Stop talking," Ma commanded with a whisper before she turned back to the officer. "Sir, your flashlight."

The man approached quickly, his eyes still skirting over the shadows as if waiting for an attack. When the beam of light focused on Marigold his attention snapped to the singular point.

"What the hell happened here?" He knelt down next to her, fingers seeking out a pulse. His eyes studied each of them in turn, suspicions clear even within the shadows.

"The ambulance is on its way," Ma interrupted the officer's thoughts.

Seemingly by will alone, Ma kept the officer's focus on Marigold as sirens broke the silence of the night.

CHAPTER 18

While the police officer might have had his suspicions, he didn't stop Louis from traveling with Marigold in the ambulance. Marigold remained unconscious for the whole journey, her skin sunken and pale in the harsh overhead light. They bombarded him with questions, a lot of which he couldn't begin to answer. For all the time they had spent together, Louis hadn't even thought to learn her blood type or if she had any allergies. He berated himself for that the entire journey.

The second the ambulance had stopped, the flurry of activity began anew. They had let him follow alongside the stretcher until they had reached the large electronic doors of the emergency room entrance. The hospital was small, only consisting of two stories and situated within the center of a garden that had thrived under loving care. At the door, he was stopped by a nurse and asked to go through the main entrance only a few feet away. The doctors needed the room to work. Louis had nodded even as he had barely heard the words, his eyes trained on the few people that surrounded Marigold as she disappeared down the hallway.

It was still before dawn, but the whole world looked brighter. The fog didn't stretch this far beyond the bayou and, without it to compete with, even the light of the streetlamps were enough to burn his eyes. Louis paced back and forth, raking his hands over the back of his head as he struggled to think of what he should do next. It was only a few moments before the police cruiser pulled up, but each one strummed through until his skin felt as tight as a bow string. The tires were still rolling when Ma jumped out of the front seat.

"She's still unconscious," Louis blurted.

Officer Brown got out of the car and quickly eyed the conversation that the two of them were having. Given the situation, the police officer hadn't been able to separate all the people involved, so questioning each of them individually hadn't been an option. Louis could see that it didn't sit right with the stocky man. Brown's shoulders looked even wider as he put his hands on his hips and looked at the mother and son.

"We still have a few things to go over," he said.

"Of course," Ma said smoothly. "We're not going anywhere, officer. We couldn't possibly leave Marigold alone."

Brown opened the back door of the police car, letting Cordelia and Rene shuffle out.

"How is she?" Cordelia asked instantly.

"They don't think there's any internal bleeding, but the ER staff are still checking on her." Louis turned to Brown. "Can we go see her now?"

"Of course," Brown said crisply. He waved his hand out before him, indicating that they take the lead.

He wanted to keep them all in eyesight. Ma grabbed Louis's hand and hurriedly pulled him faster than the rest of the group. It created just enough distance for her to whisper unheard.

"Do you have the demon's name?"

"No."

"That makes this harder."

Louis glanced to her. "But possible. Right?"

They rushed through the doorway into the hospital, the slow-moving doors hitting their shoulders as they squeezed through the emerging gap. Ma's jaw twitched as she kept her eyes straight ahead.

"I'm going to need you to get me a few things."

***

The hospital's ER was efficient but still a longer process than Louis had expected. From what he could gather, the doctors were far more concerned about Marigold's inability to regain consciousness than they were about her legs. They were organizing a CT scan. Given the hour and the limited facilities of the hospital, the process wasn't instantaneous. Louis had been grateful. It had given him some extra time to gather up the items his mother needed.

While Cordelia was the master at distracting people, Rene had proven to be pretty amazing at gathering information. He had found out that there was going to be a shift change shortly. It would leave a window of opportunity of about fifteen to twenty minutes when only the skeleton staff would be actively moving about the area.

Marigold, now considered to be in a stable condition, had been moved into one of the back rooms to await further tests. Louis had always heard of the rituals taking hours and had no idea if they could compress it into a shorter form. Perhaps Ma's strength would be enough to make it successful. If they didn't get this done now, they might have to wait days for another chance.

Rene served as a lookout, helping Louis cross the open area of the waiting room and get through the swinging double doors unseen. The hallway was already deserted and he ran down it as fast as he could, the items almost slipping from his hands with each step. Ma opened the door as he approached and he hurried through.

He dumped the items on the end of Marigold's bed and spared her a quick glance. His stomach twisted in knots at the sight. She was clean and dry, the gash on her forehead now wrapped in a pristine bandage. But it hadn't brought any color back to her face. Her lips were now pale, almost white, and dark circles surrounded each eye.

"I got everything, but I had to make some substitutions."

"Substitutions?"

"It's early morning in rural Louisiana. My options were the garden outside and a self-serve gift shop. Neither had a good voodoo section."

"This isn't voodoo," Ma corrected with a sharp edge. "To counter what you've done, I'll have to do a variation on an ancient Babylonian ritual. I'll need each item exactly."

Louis blinked at her. "They didn't even have name-brand candy."

Letting her frustration out in a heavy sigh, Ma pulled over a small rolling table that had been stripped of all surgical tools.

"Let's just get started. Do you have the bowl?"

He quickly handed over the metal bowl he had snagged from the café's kitchen. She placed it on the rolling table. When she dumped in the flour he had brought, it created a little white cloud. It drifted lazily down to coat the pristine metal as Ma closed her eyes and lifted her hands. The room began to fill with static charge. Small currents of energy sparked against each hair on his body. The sensation added to the chill in Louis's stomach as Ma held out one hand to him.

"Iron," she commanded.

He placed his now dead mobile in her palm. Instantly, her eyes opened and she glared at the device.

"Phones don't have iron in them."

"The batteries do," Louis argued. "Don't they?"

"You couldn't find anything else?"

"What else has iron in it?"

"Door handles."

"This is a new building," he argued. "All the handles are stainless steel or plastic."

Ma clenched her mouth and slapped the phone down into the flour, releasing another puffed cloud. Once her anger simmered down, she focused on the task again. Tiny dents began to litter the flour, as if it were being struck with a thousand needles at once. She whispered the words of the ritual to herself, concentrating on pronouncing instead of volume. Louis had never heard Ancient Babylonian before and had no idea how successful she was in producing the foreign sounds.

"Roots."

That one had actually be easy to find, given the amount of mulch that had clung to all of them after they had pulled Rene and Marigold free from the bayou. Ma seemed satisfied enough as she wound the grass around the phone.

"The feather."

Louis cringed as he offered up the only thing he had been able to find. It was a bright pink novelty pen shaped to look like a flamingo. Its body was covered in a thick tuff of tiny feathers that he was pretty sure were real. Ma narrowed her eyes on the item, hovering between astonished and enraged.

"The gardeners here are really dedicated to keeping the yard clean," he mumbled by way of an apology.

Ma snatched the pen out of his hand and yanked out a few of the feathers before tossing the rest of it aside.

Her eyes were cool as she asked, "How about the animal fur?"

Louis cringed and held up the only thing he had been able to find. "Wool socks?"

"Wool is the sheep's fur," he defended.

"Louis, we need to get this done now. It's only going to get harder if the demon wakes up within her."

"I know," he hissed. "But it was all I could find. It's not the best, but with your strength behind it, it should still work. Right?"

"I have limitations, Louis," she snapped even as she took the socks.

She threaded the feathers into the folds of the knitted wool and wrapped them both around the phone before she placed them back into the bowl. The flour once again stirred as an unseen force slithered like snakes under the surface. Ma's lips never stopped moving but Louis couldn't hear a word. The silence was disturbed only by the soft, rhythmic beeping of the heart monitor. Louis didn't move a muscle until Ma opened her eyes and looked over to him.

"I take it that you couldn't find a wax or clay vessel for demons."

Louis sheepishly lifted up a lime green plush giraffe. Ma didn't hesitate to reach out to take it, resigned to the uphill struggle. She moved closer to Marigold's bedside, giraffe in hand, leaving the small table behind. Louis remained at the end of the bed, watching, unsure what he was supposed to do. He had never witnessed this ritual before but could already feel the heat it created. Steam rose up in the bowl as if it were filled with dry ice. It trickled over the rim and pooled against the table.

Ma spoke again, a gentle murmur of words before she abruptly spat on Marigold's head. Using her thumb, she spread the liquid out across Marigold's brow before repeating the process with the giraffe. The steam from the bowl grew thicker as it released a sweltering heat into the room. Louis watched as it thickened and grew, becoming long twisted tentacles that unfurled from the edges of the bowl and stretched out to coil around Ma's legs.

Speaking in a continuous whisper, Ma spat on Marigold's hands and sternum, once again mirroring the actions with the plush toy. The smoke tendrils coiled over Ma's hips and wrapped around her waist as she worked. They never hindered her as she moved. Louis backed away for Ma to take his place at the foot of the bed. She pulled the sheets back, exposing Marigold's engorged and discolored feet. Louis had to look away, his throat swelling closed at the sight of what he had done.

Ma spat on both of Marigold's feet and then turned to complete the process with the toy. The second her spit hit the giraffe's left foot, Marigold jerked. Her left foot spun until it released a sickening crack, a sound Louis knew all too well. The bone had broken again, her foot twisting until it pointed backwards. He ran to Marigold's side. She was still asleep.

He grabbed her right leg, holding it tightly as Ma completed the spit ritual with the giraffe's foot. It didn't matter. The limb moved within his grasp, his fingers uselessly sliding over the flesh. With a crack that matched the first, her foot turned until her toes pressed into the mattress. Louis reeled back, turning his eyes to his mother. The tendrils now rose above her, expanding out in all directions, filling the space until they brushed against the ceiling and the walls.

Louis backed away, his heart hammering in his chest. Each breath brought the static charge of the air deep into his lungs until he trembled from the force. Ma ignored them, continuing undisturbed in her mumble of words. With both hands, she raised the plush toy high over her head and brought it down like a driving stake onto the bed. The second it made contact, the tentacles struck. They burrowed deep into her stomach and pulled, yanking her up until her spine almost folded in half.

"Hold her down," Ma commanded.

Louis leaped on top of Marigold, attempting to use his weight to drive her back down against the mattress. His presence barely made a difference. Her bones creaked with the effort and she began to thrash. Ma continued unhindered as he fought to keep Marigold from injuring herself. The struggle bucked and threw Louis, leaving him scrambling to keep his hold. He never felt any of the tentacles that remained probing and tugging inside of her. He only felt the power they exerted.

With his forearm across her chest, he bore down with the entirety of his weight until her shoulders were flush with the mattress again. Draped over her still thrashing form, Louis couldn't catch his breath. His lungs cracked as his mother's power increased. It felt like sucking in electricity itself. The lights overhead buzzed, the heart monitor flicking on and off in a way that was sure to draw attention. He glanced back at his mother, searching for guidance, and found the woman now suspended in the air, drawn up by the squirming tendrils that now covered every inch of space.

Marigold screamed and Louis clamped his hand over her mouth, trying to force her jaw shut. The sound continued, muffled but strong. He turned to her and felt his heart stop. She was watching him. He felt her gaze sink into him, slithering around something deep in his core and reeling him in. It felt like he was falling, tumbling through an endless nothingness, as her eyes grew before him. The tiny veins within the whites of her eyes became a towering forest before him. Blood swelled within each one until they burst and flooded the surrounding area.

The air rushed from his lungs as something else took hold of him. It wrapped around him and hurled Louis back from the bloody forest. He felt himself fall into his skin before he was sent flying across the room. His back slammed against the wall, his brain rattling within his skull as he tried to make sense of what had just happened.

Ma rose higher into the air, her attention focused on Marigold as everything within the room began to rattle. The heat increased until it burned Louis's skin. Marigold sat upright, no longer glaring at the woman with eyes, but with circular pools of blood. The demon was trying to draw Ma in, just as it had done so easily to Louis. But Ma only stared back as the tentacles drove into Marigold like a thousand daggers.

Louis bolted for the door and pressed his back against it, attempting to keep anyone out as the energy grew. The floor continued to heat until the wheels of the rolling table and bed began to melt. Sweat drenched his clothes. It felt like his very marrow was boiling. Marigold continued to stare, but it had no effect on Ma. The pure liquid orbs of her eyes began to leak, dripping down over her face until there were only gaping holes where her eyes had once been. Ma continued her chanting. The walls rattled until they threatened to burst. The contents of the bowl exploded into a thousand fireworks.

Louis shielded his face as he pulled into a crouch. The soles of his shoes had melted into thick goo and the plastic of his glasses began to soften and burn against his skin. He longed to pull them off but feared to lose his sight. Marigold opened her mouth to release a scream, but the smoke poured inside. She choked and thrashed, struggling to breathe as the smoke encased her and forced her back down against the mattress.

The plush giraffe was flung into the air. Ma latched onto its neck with one hand. Cracks formed in the window glass and the paint began to melt as Ma spoke the final words. Marigold tried to scream again as Ma grabbed the giraffes head with her free hand. She twisted and ripped the toy in two. Blood spurted out from it, soaking Ma's hands and dripping down onto the floor that her feet didn't touch. The sound of ripping flesh turned Louis's stomach. Marigold screamed, blood seeping out from around the smoke that clogged her throat. Ma didn't take her eyes away from Marigold as she threw the remains of the toy into the crackling, raging fire within the bowl. It consumed the fabric within seconds. Marigold bellowed as much as she was able, her spine twisting, her limbs trembling. When the last inch of material was lost to the flames, she flopped back down against the mattress, blood-drenched and as still as the dead.

***

Louis jerked away when someone touched his shoulder. Blinking blearily, he looked up to see his mother smiling down at him. Fatigue had claimed him soon after the ritual had been conducted. They had barely enough time to slip out before the change of shift had arrived. It seemed that the chaos had been completely contained within the one room. No one outside had heard anything, seen anything, even felt a change in the temperature as far as he was aware. Rene had been able to piece together a bit of the chatter. They hadn't been able to clean Marigold before they left, and the running theory amongst the doctors was a burst capillary or aneurism.

Losing her eyes entirely, however, had been a trick, most likely to play on Ma's sympathy and make her stop. The demon obviously didn't know Louis's Ma very well.

It hadn't taken long for Ma to fall asleep in the waiting room. Louis had been able to hold off until Marigold was out of the emergency CT scans and x-rays. They had wheeled her into the room, both legs set in thick casts and suspended by dangling ropes. The second she was situated, Louis had pulled a chair up to her bedside. He remembered sitting down, but nothing after that.

"What time it is?" he asked as he glanced over at Marigold.

A little bit of color had seeped back into her cheeks and her hand now felt warm under his, but it didn't seem like she had moved an inch.

"A bit after eight," Ma said.

"Are you okay?" he asked, unable to suppress his yawn.

"Still a bit sleepy. I'm waiting for her to wake up to see if I can go get a hotel room nearby. I'm too old for waiting room chairs."

Louis smirked. "After last night, I wouldn't have thought so."

"It was stupid of you to look it in the eye," Ma said.

"I've done a few stupid things," Louis admitted. He smiled at his mother, letting true warmth and gratitude seep out from behind his fatigue. "Thank you."

"Don't thank me until we see what state she's in," Ma said.

Louis's throat clenched. "But the ritual worked right?"

"I can't be certain. But even if it's gone, there might still be some lasting damage."

Trying to hide the quiver in his voice, he glanced at her, "What do you mean?"

"Black magic isn't just dangerous because of what it summons," she said.
"There is no certainty in it. The same spell can have a thousand different reactions that the human body just isn't built to withstand. I won't be able to judge what we've actually done to her until she wakes up. Although, something must be said about the doctors being so hopeful." Ma allowed a long moment of silence to linger before she spoke again. "You really messed up, Louis."

"I know."

"If I hadn't already been on my way."

"I know," Louis repeated.

She sucked in an audible breath, swallowing down her simmering anger. "I don't think that the police officer believes us. He's growing suspicious."

Louis didn't answer. He just squeezed Marigold's hand, begging for some kind of sign that she was in there. She didn't move.

"We're sticking to the story that she fell. Admittedly, it's not the best, but we've already committed to it. Louis, are you paying attention?"

"Yes."

"I want to hear you say it."

"She fell," he said numbly.

"One more time with a little conviction."

Louis cleared his throat and pushed out the words again. They still felt flat against his tongue but were solid enough to satisfy her.

"You don't know anything beyond that," Ma instructed. "Don't try and elaborate. You're a horrible liar."

"I know."

"She'll be okay," Ma assured as she squeezed his shoulder again. "Or we'll keep fighting until she is."

His mother was at the door by the time he could trust himself to speak.

"Thanks, Ma. Why don't you get a hotel room?"

"I don't want to go too far."

"That would be impossible. This town barely has more than three blocks. Besides, she'll be in no condition to go anywhere." He hesitated over the last words. "And we might need you well rested."

She nodded once, her fingers clenching the doorframe to keep in all the things she didn't want to say at the moment. It was just a matter of time before her rage came up and he had to face the enormity of her anger. He had used dark magic. He had almost killed someone. He had almost gotten all of them killed. These were not things that she was going to let go. But for now, she swallowed her words and left him alone to his personal demons without comment.

Louis slid down a little further in his seat and let his eyes drift close. *Everything will be fine,* he told himself as he started to drift. It was a lot easier to believe it as the morning light drifted through the hospital room windows. There was a steady strum of workers bustling around outside the door, proof that life existed, that they weren't alone. The beeping of her heart monitor created a lullaby that lured him deeper into sleep. He slumped against the chair, comforted by the warm, smooth skin covering the back of Marigold's hand that suddenly twitched.

Louis bolted upright to find Marigold smiling at him, her eyes open, a pristine blue. A sob wretched from his throat. He couldn't tell if it was one of guilt or relief. But her fingers entwined with his and she reached for him with her free hand. He fell into her, wrapping one arm carefully but tightly around her waist as he buried his face in the crook of her neck. She held him back just as tightly, her fingers clutching the material of his shirt.

"I'm so sorry," he said, only to be gently shushed into silence.

They held each other for a long moment, the warmth of her body easing the aches of his muscles.

"It's going to be okay," he promised. "Everything will be better now."

"Thank you, Louis."

Ice flooded through his body as the word hit his ear.

His name.

Spoken with the perfect French emphasis.

He had his hand still against her spine, and his heart stuttered when he felt the bones move. Louis took in a sharp breath, unsure if the sensation was just a trick of his sleep-drenched mind or real. He was still mulling over the question when, suddenly, sharp nails raked across the skin of his palm. He wrenched his hand back and stared at Marigold. She didn't let go. Didn't move. It could have been a trick.

Safe and warm, surrounded by light, he could believe that he wasn't holding a demon. All he had to do was ignore the pain that still streaked along his palm.

* * *

If you enjoyed the book, please leave a review. Your reviews inspire us to continue writing about the world of spooky and untold horrors!

Check out these best-selling books from our talented authors

Ron Ripley (Ghost Stories)
- Berkley Street Series Books 1 – 9
  www.scarestreet.com/berkleyfullseries
- Moving in Series Box Set Books 1 – 6
  www.scarestreet.com/movinginboxfull

A. I. Nasser (Supernatural Suspense)
- Slaughter Series Books 1 – 3 Bonus Edition
  www.scarestreet.com/slaughterseries

David Longhorn (Sci-Fi Horror)
- Nightmare Series: Books 1 – 3
  www.scarestreet.com/nightmarebox
- Nightmare Series: Books 4 – 6
  www.scarestreet.com/nightmare4-6

Sara Clancy (Supernatural Suspense)
- Banshee Series Books 1 – 6
  www.scarestreet.com/banshee1-6

For a complete list of our new releases and best-selling horror books, visit www.scarestreet.com/books

See you in the shadows,
Team Scare Street

Printed in Great Britain
by Amazon

49135650R00093